BILLIONAIRE'S BABY

PAMELA M. KELLEY

PIPING PLOVER PRESS

~Author Note~

**The name of one of the characters, Adiel, is pronounced, Ah Dee El. I have a friend with that name, who is also a filmmaker and I've always loved the sound of it—it fits this character perfectly. :)

CHAPTER 1

Anna Kelley held her breath as she slid open the envelope from University of Idaho, the last of the law schools that she was waiting to hear from. She'd applied to five others, with U Idaho being her 'safety' school. It wasn't her first choice, but she had the best shot of getting into it in case the others said no. And they'd all said no. U Idaho was her last chance. She opened the letter and breathed a sigh of relief.

"What are you looking so happy about?" Her stepmother, Elise Cummings, walked into the kitchen and poured herself a cup of coffee. She was on her way to work as the office manager of Powers and Thompson, Riston's largest law firm. As usual, she looked like she'd just walked out of a fashion magazine. Her pale blonde hair fell sharply to her chin, and her royal blue dress and high heels showed off her perfect figure and showcased toned calves. A strand of icy pearls completed the look.

Anna glanced down at her own faded sweats and pushed back a wavy piece of hair that had escaped her messy ponytail. Today, of all days, she was not going to allow Elise to make her feel less-than. She lifted her chin and smiled.

"I just got some good news. University of Idaho accepted me to law school. I'll be able to commute from here, which will save money. I'm excited."

"Hmmm. You may want to open your other letter. Looks like it just arrived today." Anna followed Elise's gaze to the white envelope that sat next to the one from U Idaho. Anna hadn't even noticed it. She turned her attention to it now and recognized the return address.

"It's from the law firm where you work?"

Elise nodded. "Yes, they are handling your father's estate and drew up his will."

Her father had died several weeks ago after a long illness. Anna was still grieving his death, but he'd been sick for so long that when he finally passed, there was a sense of relief, too, that his suffering was over.

Anna relaxed a little. "It's just a formality, then? I know what's in my father's will."

"You may want to take a look. Your father revised his will shortly before he died." There was a gleam in Elise's eye that Anna didn't like. She'd seen that look before and it was never good news. Elise was not a good person, and she'd never hidden the fact that she hated Anna. She had what some might consider a good reason, but Anna had always hoped that eventually, Elise would forgive her. With a pit in her stomach, she ripped open the envelope. And when she looked up, there were tears in eyes as she faced Elise.

"How could you do this?"

Elise stirred some sugar into her coffee before saying, "Whatever do you mean? Your father just did what he thought best. For all of us. But, it doesn't look like there will be any money for law school. And I think it's best if you move out. I want to turn your bedroom into an office. But, I'm not completely heartless. I'll give you thirty days."

"How did you convince him to do this?" Anna's father had been very sick for years, and the past six months he'd been bedridden and confused as his memory deteriorated.

"It wasn't hard. I just told him that you'd received full scholarships to the schools you applied to, so you didn't need his money, but we did. After all his medical expenses, there's really not much left. Just enough to keep the house going and to pay for school for Tommy and Hayley when it's time for them to go."

"I could fight this. He wasn't in his right mind." Anna knew her stepmother hated her, but she'd never known how much.

"You could," Elise agreed. "But you'd need to hire a lawyer and that costs money. And do you really want to deprive your siblings of the chance to go to school? You once told me that you'd do anything to make up for what you did. Do you remember that?"

Anna had said that, and she'd meant it. "Yes, I remember that."

"So, it's settled, then. I have to run or I'll be late. Have a great day." She smiled sweetly and then breezed out the door.

The tears came hard as soon as Anna was alone. She thought she was done crying over her father, but this brought everything up again and she cried like she'd never cried before, letting it all out. She knew her father didn't want this. Once the tears finally stopped, she poured herself a fresh cup of coffee and tried to figure out what to do next.

"Do you want scrambled with cheese or over easy?"

Ben was deep into the problem he was trying to work out and his housekeeper, Betty Higgins, interrupted his train of thought.

"I'm not hungry," he said, trying to keep the irritation out of his voice. His stomach betrayed him by growling a moment later.

Betty smiled and he could tell she was trying not to laugh. He was lucky to have her. She was a retired schoolteacher and her children lived all over the country. Being a live-in housekeeper kept her busy and he could tell she enjoyed the work, having someone to look after.

"Fine. I'll have scrambled with cheese."

He was sitting at the expansive, marble-topped island in his kitchen. There was a soft cooing sound coming from the chair next to him and he leaned over to take a peek. His eleven-month-old niece Taylor was sleeping peacefully. One of her feet poked out of the baby blanket. Even though she was wearing soft cashmere booties, he readjusted the blanket and tucked it securely around both feet. He rubbed his eyes and gratefully nodded when Betty came over with more coffee.

"Late night?" she asked as she set down a plate of eggs, potatoes and toast in front of him.

"I didn't sleep much last night," he admitted as he tucked into the breakfast.

"I picked this up for you." She handed him a tube of gel.

He looked at the label and raised his eyebrows. "Baby Teething Gel?"

"She's teething. That's why she's crying as much as she is. It hurts. Rub a little of that along her gums and it will ease the pain."

"Thanks. I will."

"Any luck finding some nanny candidates?" Betty had been after him since the day he'd hired her six weeks ago to get a live-in nanny as soon as possible. She'd said he couldn't do it all himself and he knew she was right. He'd had part-time help in Silicon Valley and was still exhausted. He knew he needed someone full-time, but wanted to wait until he was all settled into the new place in Riston.

"Yes, I have four I'm going to set up interviews with."

"Good. I have another suggestion, if you don't mind."

He chuckled. He knew she was going to share her opinion whether he minded or not.

"Don't interview them here."

That surprised him. He'd planned on having them out to the ranch. It was an impressive property with several hundred acres, a sprawling five-bedroom main house and a caretaker's cottage, which is where Mrs. Higgins lived. It was a gorgeous home, with white columns out front and a wrap-around porch. The office where he'd planned to interview the nannies was plush, with a working fireplace, built-in mahogany wood cabinets and the entry way was the same rich marble used in the kitchen countertop.

"You don't want them to know how wealthy I am?"

She nodded. "You're not just wealthy. You're a billionaire, Ben, and you're in your early thirties and not half-bad looking. I'm just looking out for you. You want a nanny that is here for her, not for you."

"Smart thinking. That didn't even cross my mind. I suppose it should have." Ben still wasn't used to the word billionaire. It didn't seem real. Yet, he wasn't just a billionaire, he was a multi-billionaire. He'd started out as a lawyer for a venture capital firm. Then the entrepreneurial bug bit and he left to help grow a start-up social media company with cutting-edge technology his college roommate developed. Ben came on as CEO and helped take the company public. Once they figured out how to monetize the technology, through online advertising, it was like they turned on a money faucet with no off switch.

"So, where do you think I should meet them?"

It was clear that Betty had thought this through. "Why don't you meet them at that cute coffee and ice cream shop at River's End Ranch, Sadie's Saloon?"

Ben hadn't been there yet, but had heard the coffee and ice cream was outstanding. Still, it seemed like an odd, out of the way place. He'd expected her to say somewhere along Main Street.

"Why there?"

"You can kill two birds with one stone. It's a short walk to the Kids' Korral. You can stop in there and check it out. It's an excellent day care and they do babysitting, too. You need an emergency back-up plan for Taylor in case your nanny or I am not around. Plus, if you schedule them in the afternoon, it's not busy then, so you won't be bothered. You'll be taking Taylor, of course."

He nodded. "Yes, I thought they should meet her and see who they'll be caring for." They were quiet for a minute and then he laughed, realizing another reason she'd picked that spot. "If she gets fussy, she won't be bothering too many people. That's brilliant."

Mrs. Higgins looked pleased by the compliment.

"Finish your eggs. You've got some interviews to schedule."

He winked at her. "Yes, ma'am."

ANNA'S BEST FRIEND, Tammy Burns, was already sitting at a table at Sadie's Saloon when Anna arrived. Anna joined her at the table and Tammy pushed a tall to-go cup of coffee towards her.

"I ordered for you. Caramel nut, black, one sugar."

"Thank you." Anna looked around the cozy shop. There were a few people in line for coffees and only one other table was occupied. It was the table next to theirs and there was just one man, with his back to them, and a baby carrier on the chair next to him.

"You're right, this place has the best coffee. I've been coming here just about every afternoon since I started at Melissa's shop." Tammy was the assistant manager for the bookstore at the ranch, since the owner, who was also a published author, wanted to spend more time on her writing.

"How's it going so far? Do you still love it?" Tammy graduated the year before Anna and as an English major, she'd had a hard time finding interesting work in Riston. She wasn't able to leave Riston for several years due to family issues and had almost given up and was about to take a waitress position when the opportunity came up to work with Melissa. Anna was thrilled for her.

"I do. I'm going to miss our current assistant though. She's been great, and she was with Melissa since she opened."

"She's going to graduate school?" Anna thought that was what she remembered.

Tammy nodded. "She's going to UCLA to get her MBA."

A thought occurred to Anna. "Will you need to hire someone to replace her?"

"No. I'm sorry. I wish we could. But Melissa hired me knowing Anna was leaving. I'll just be working more shifts than she did and Melissa will be in the rest of the time."

"Okay." Anna took the lid off her coffee to help it cool more quickly and leaned over to inhale its aroma. It smelled like comfort, warm and toasty. She took a sip and tried not to think about her situation, which was growing more distressing by the day.

"How are you doing? Anything look promising?"

The concern and worry in her voice made Anna's eyes well up. Tammy was truly the only person left who cared about her.

"I'm hanging in there. But no one seems to be hiring and I've been applying for anything and everything. There just isn't much out there."

"How much time do you have left?"

"Two weeks before I'm supposed to be out."

"Well, I talked to my mother, and she said you're welcome to stay with us for as long as you need to."

"Thank you. I really appreciate that." Tammy lived with her mother and their place was a tiny two-bedroom. If Anna stayed there, she'd be sleeping on their living room sofa and she didn't mind, but she didn't want to disrupt their house. She'd do it if she needed to, but it was a last, though very welcome, resort.

An older woman with silvery white hair and dancing blue eyes stopped by their table. She'd just bought a coffee and looked like she was on her way out.

"I thought that was you, dear. Who is your friend?"

Tammy's face lit up when she saw the older lady. "Hi, Jaclyn. This is Anna. We've been best friends since third grade."

Anna held out her hand. "It's very nice to meet you."

Jaclyn held onto her hand and looked deep into her eyes as if she was searching for something. She finally nodded and let go of her hand.

"Lovely to meet you dear. The fairies were right again. They always are. Enjoy your coffee and may I suggest you get a refill and relax a spell. You are where you are supposed to be."

Anna's jaw dropped. Tammy had told her about Jaclyn, the eccentric older woman who lived by the RV park in a yard filled with garden gnomes and dozens of white rabbits that followed her everywhere, even into the house. She also said she was very sweet and perfectly normal except for the messages she received every now and then that she said came from fairies. The legend also went that Jaclyn and her fairies had a hand in match-making all of the Weston siblings, and many of their cousins and friends.

"I have to run. Simon won't be happy if his coffee is cold when I get there." Jaclyn headed off to deliver the coffee. But before she left, she had one parting comment. "I hope we'll see you at trivia tonight?" She turned Anna's way. "You should come too, dear. It's a lot of fun and will get your mind off things. Bye, now."

"So, that's Jaclyn," Anna said.

"The one and only. You really should come to trivia tonight. Jaclyn's right. It will get your mind off everything."

"Maybe I will. How does she know that, though? I couldn't make sense of half of what she was talking about."

"That's just Jaclyn. Maybe it will become more clear, or not. One never knows." Tammy laughed, and then glanced at the clock and stood up.

"I have to get back to the shop."

Anna stood to go, too, and went to put the lid back on her coffee.

"Don't rush out on my account. Why not take Jaclyn's advice and stay and relax? Sadie makes awesome ice cream. Treat yourself to the sea salt caramel fudge ripple. It's to die for."

"Maybe I will. That does sound good." Anna got in line to get an ice cream as Tammy left.

BEN WATCHED AS TAYLOR STRETCHED, yawned and then fell fast asleep again. He'd fed her when he first arrived here, so if all went well he'd have at least an hour or so to talk to four nannies before she woke up. He scheduled them fifteen minutes apart and stressed that it was important that they show up at their exact designated time, not five minutes before or after. According to his watch, nanny number one was due to arrive in one minute.

"Ben Turner?"

He turned at the brusque voice. A woman in her early fifties stood before him, with mostly gray hair that was scraped into a severe bun. Thick black glasses, a gray cardigan, black pants and sensible shoes completed the outfit. He stood and held out his hand. "You must be Abigail Green? Please have a seat."

She sat across from him and folded her hands together in front of her, like a steeple.

"Thank you for coming. So, Miss Green, your resume is impressive. You've worked with children for many years. I've noticed that your recent positions didn't last for more than a few months?"

"That is correct. How do you young people say it? We weren't on the same page regarding disciplining the children." Abigail pressed her lips together in a firm line as if she found the line of questioning distasteful. Too bad.

"Could you explain that please?"

"I don't believe in babying children. I do believe in structure, rules, and consequences if those rules are broken."

"Okay. Here's a situational question. If a baby cries, what do you do?"

"Assuming I know that nothing is wrong—well, I let the baby cry, of course. Eventually, they stop."

"Are you saying that if my baby, Taylor here, cried, you would not pick her up to comfort her?"

Abigail scoffed. "No, probably not. Unless I suspected something was wrong with the child. Otherwise, I don't believe in spoiling them."

"I see. Well, I thank you for coming. I will be in touch."

"Thank you for your time as well."

Abigail left and Ben ripped her resume in half. Whoever he hired would cuddle his Taylor whenever she needed to be comforted. He had a few minutes before the next candidate, so he decided to get a refill on his coffee. On his way back to his table, he noticed the pretty blonde woman sitting behind him. He hadn't seen her come in before as his back was to her, but he'd overheard her talking to her friend about looking for a job.

He doubted she'd be interested in a live-in nanny position, though. She didn't look the type. She had long, stylish hair, and was wearing trendy jeans, well-worn cowboy boots and a very flattering light blue sweater that showed off her shapely curves. It was just as well. Having a live-in nanny that looked like that would be too distracting.

"You the guy looking to hire a nanny?"

Ben turned at the laid-back voice and almost dropped his coffee.

"Angel Givens?"

"That's me."

Ben asked her to sit down and tried not to stare at the piercing in her nose, or the one in her eyebrow or the one in the middle of her lip. It was hard to know where to look. Her blonde hair was shaggy and fell to her shoulders. The last inch of her hair was dyed green which helped to give her an overall otherworldly look. Denim overalls and a rainbow tie-dyed shirt added to the colorful picture.

"So, tell me about yourself," he asked.

Angel shrugged. "Not much to tell. You need someone to watch your kid. I can do that."

"You've worked as a nanny before?" Ben ruffled through his papers and found her resume. She didn't have a lot of experience but she had worked at a daycare center and for a private family, though now that he looked more closely he saw the red flags that he'd missed earlier. She was only at the day care center for about six months and the private family's last name was also Givens.

"I have. I sent in a resume." Her tone was slightly defensive and prompted Ben to ask, "Why did you leave the day care center?"

She scowled. "They let me go."

"Oh? why?"

"They said I called out sick too many times and was late too often. I really wasn't, though." She lifted her chin defiantly and Ben sighed. He had one final question before he ended the interview.

"Are you related to the Givens family on your resume?"

Angel smirked. "That's a good guess."

"So you didn't really work as a nanny for our own family?"

Angel shrugged. "I watched my younger sister now and then. Close enough right? I had to put something on my resume."

"How old was your sister? Have you ever cared for an infant?"

Angel wrinkled her nose. "My sister is ten now. And I don't do diapers. Never have, never will."

"Okay. Well, my niece is a baby. She needs a little help still. I'm afraid this isn't a good fit."

Angel stood and shrugged again. "Fine by me. See ya."

As Angel walked off, Ben felt a bit of panic rising. He hoped that nanny number three would be better. If she was relatively normal, he was inclined to hire her on the spot. These three were the best resumes he'd received. He'd been sure that he'd be able to cross hiring a nanny off his to-do list. Even though he'd stepped down as CEO, he was still the largest shareholder and an adviser to the company he helped found, and there was a steady stream of work and phone calls involved with that.

"Well, hello there." A gorgeous, petite blonde woman stood before him. She wore a tailored cream-colored dress that fit her maybe just a little too snugly so that it was very clear that she had not an ounce of extra fat on her very toned figure. Her hair was shoulder length and styled into a fluffy mane of curls. Her heels were so high he wondered how she managed to walk in them.

"Nadine Johnson?" She looked like she was ready for a date instead of an interview.

"That's me!"

"Please, have a seat." He found her resume and went through her experience with her. She had the best experience so far. It appeared that she'd worked for several local families during school and summers. But something about her just seemed not quite right.

"We're so glad that you've moved here," she gushed.

"Oh, why's that?"

"Well, you're so famous and you've done so much. I hear that you bought the old Wellington Ranch. That is a beautiful property. Is that where we will be living?"

She sounded very, very eager to move in. And now Ben knew what bothered him.

"Yes, this is a live-in position. Do you think your boyfriend would have a problem with that?"

She leaned forward and smiled. "I'm totally single, so that won't be a problem."

Ben was desperate, so against his better judgment, he gave her another chance to prove herself, but he was fairly sure of how she'd answer.

"I think Taylor needs a diaper change. Would you mind taking her into the rest room and changing it for her? I have a diaper right here." He went to reach in Taylor's bag for a diaper, but Nadine was already on her feet. She looked as though she was going to be sick.

"I'm sorry, but I have to run. I hope to hear from you soon."

He sighed with relief as she tottered out on her high heels, going so fast he was sure she'd fall over.

"Mr. Turner?" A polite voice enquired. Ben turned and smiled. Finally, a proper nanny had arrived.

"You must be Emily Pearson. It's a pleasure to meet you. Please have a seat."

But instead, the preppy young woman with the navy skirt, white sweater, matching headband and a perky ponytail bit her lip and looked uncomfortable.

"I'm so sorry. I got the phone call on my way here

to meet you so wanted to tell you in person. I've just received and accepted a job offer, so I won't be able to interview for your nanny position. I'm moving to Manhattan—this is my dream position. I hope you understand."

Ben sighed. He did understand. All too well. "Of course, and I thank you for telling me in person." He smiled. "You don't by any chance know any nannies you could recommend?"

Emily bit her lip again. "I'm so sorry. I don't. Good luck, Mr. Turner."

CHAPTER 2

Anna's heart went out to the man sitting behind her. By now she knew his name was Ben Turner, a name she'd heard before, but couldn't place. She'd also noticed when he went up for more coffee that he was very tall, well over six foot two, and he was lean, as if he worked out often. His dark brown hair was a little too long and fell over green eyes with lashes so long that it just wasn't fair. She'd seen his job listed in the local paper. It was one of the few that she hadn't applied for. A live-in situation would be perfect, but being a nanny wasn't an option for her.

His cell phone rang and two seconds later his baby woke up. The ringer must have woken her, and she was not happy about it. Soft whimpers quickly turned to screams.

"David, can I call you back? Yes, I know we agreed to talk now. Okay, if we can make it fast."

The baby screamed even louder as if she wanted everyone's attention and she got it.

"David, can you hold on just one second?" He picked up the baby, and she quieted for a moment, but when he reached for his phone, she screamed again—a piercing, murderous howl. Instinctively, Anna jumped up and held out her arms, and a baffled Ben set down the phone and passed the baby over. He watched for a moment to see what would happen and no doubt to make sure Anna didn't make a dash for the door with his baby. Anna carefully cuddled her close, and the baby let out a big, satisfied burp and then snuggled in and shut her eyes. A moment later she was fast asleep. Ben's jaw dropped.

"I think she's just a little gassy. Take your call. I'm in no hurry."

He did as she suggested and a few minutes later, ended the call and turned his attention back to the two of them. The baby was still sound asleep and Anna, for the first time in weeks, felt useful.

"Thank you. I can take her back now."

Anna handed her over, and he got her situated back in her carrier again, snug under her baby blanket.

"Please have a seat for a moment. So I can thank you properly. Can I buy you a coffee or an ice cream?"

Anna laughed. "No, thank you. I've already had plenty of both."

"How did you do that? She went to sleep so easily for you."

"I used to be really good with babies. I could tell she needed to let out some gas. She's very sweet."

His expression softened. "Thank you. I'm pretty fond of her myself." He held out his hand. "You may have already heard me say this once or twice, but I'm Ben Turner. And it's very nice to meet you."

"Anna Kelley. It is nice to meet you too and I'm sorry that you didn't have any luck finding a nanny today."

"I was feeling pretty sorry for myself, I will admit. But now that I've met you I'm wondering if my luck might be changing."

Anna laughed. "Oh, I'm sorry, but I'm not a nanny."

"That's too bad. You could be, though. Unless you already have a job?"

Anna felt her eyes grow wet, which frustrated her. She fought back the tears which she knew were there just because her emotions were so raw. She had to find a job, anything soon.

"I don't have a job. I've been looking, but—well, I haven't found the right thing yet."

"What kind of job are you looking for?"

"Just about anything," Anna admitted. "I graduated college last month, a semester early, and was hoping to start law school in the fall. But I may need to push that off a year until I get my finances sorted." She'd told the University of Idaho that she was delighted to accept but had come to the realization that she might need to defer attending for a year.

She hoped that she'd be able to come up with a plan to get the money by then. Under her family's income, she wouldn't qualify for financial aid. If she applied on her own, she should qualify but it would take some time to get that paperwork in order and she wasn't sure if she'd make it for this year. Deferring for a year would give her time to save up some money and maybe find some kind of permanent part-time job she could do while in school. She still needed to figure out where she would live, as well. It was all more than a bit overwhelming.

"It sounds like you have a lot on your plate. I do, too." He was quiet for a moment and then nodded as if a decision had been made. "Why don't you come work for me? I recently moved here from Silicon Valley. My sister was a single mother and died unexpectedly, from breast cancer that they didn't find until it was much too late. I've had Taylor now for almost six months. My priorities have changed since then. I used to be in the news a lot, because of my company, Blue Sky Pages. Maybe you've heard of it?"

Anna stared at the handsome man in front of her. So that's why he looked vaguely familiar. She hadn't made the connection before. He was *the* Ben Turner, the one whose company had exploded. He was all over the entertainment pages for his love life—he used to be seen with a different famous actress or model every other week. Now that she thought of it, though, she realized she hadn't heard a thing about his love life for months.

Probably since Taylor came into his life. He'd been on the red carpet in recent years, too, for investments in hit movies-an artsy film had even won an Oscar a year ago for best original screenplay. She remembered that because she'd loved the movie, Lilacs by the Sea, and because she was obsessed with movies. She loved movies the way Tammy loved books.

"Yes, I've heard of it. Congratulations on Lilacs by the Sea. I loved that movie."

He grinned. "You've seen it? That was a most satisfying win. The screenplay blew me away when they showed it to me."

"What is your involvement with movies like that?" She found it fascinating.

He leaned forward. "I'm sort of the money guy. I got into it because one of my best friends, Adiel Bozeman, is a show runner, actually—for Pinstripes, the legal drama on Netflix."

"What's a show runner?" Anna wasn't familiar with the term.

"He's the head writer, often the creator of the story itself and in charge of the other writers and planning the show."

"I love Pinstripes." It was one of her favorite serial dramas.

"He's crazy talented. He introduced me to a buddy

of his who had a great script but needed some funding to get a pilot made. Amazon studios picked up that one, and it kind of went from there. I do maybe one or two projects like that a year. Though I may do more now that I'm out of Silicon Valley."

"Are you planning to stay here in Riston?" It seemed like such a change from his exciting life in California.

He nodded. "Yes. I'd like to. It's been a lot of fun, but the pace is crazy and I'm too visible there. There's too much attention on me and I just don't want that anymore. I want a quieter life and I love it here. People don't care about any of that."

"That's true. Most people here are very nice." Aside from Elise Cummings, that was.

"Listen, Anna, this could be a good solution for both of us. I need a nanny immediately. You need a job and you're great with my baby. Why don't we give it a try and see how it goes? The pay is pretty good." He mentioned a weekly salary amount that made Anna's jaw drop. There was nothing else she could do that would pay as well.

"Oh, and you'll have two nights off per week to yourself."

"When do you want me to start?"

"I'm supposed to start on Monday," Anna said softly

so that only Tammy could hear. There were about twelve people gathered around a big round table to play trivia. Jaclyn was on the other side of her, along with Simon. Wade Weston, the general manager of River's End Ranch, sat next to him, and then Bernie and Lily who worked in the office with him, and Barbi who used to be their waitress on trivia night, but now she ran her yoga studio full-time. Wade's friend, Clark Baker, was there too, sitting next to Tammy.

Anna had been to trivia with them a few times before, but hadn't met Clark yet. He was just as Tammy described, tall and charming. He was an orthopedics doctor and Anna could swear Tammy seemed a little flustered as she spoke to him. He was very handsome and Anna found this quite interesting as she'd never seen Tammy the slightest bit nervous, about anything.

"Well, that's great news. You're not having second thoughts are you?" Tammy asked.

Anna was having serious second thoughts.

"I am. I mean it sounds great, and the salary is almost too good to be true, but you know it's not the right job for me. I have no business being a nanny."

"I know why you feel that way, and I get it, but I don't agree. I happen to think you'd make a great nanny. Kids love you. They always have."

"It's not that easy."

"Sure it is." Jaclyn patted Anna's arm and Anna jumped. She thought they'd been so quiet.

"I don't think you understand. It's complicated," Anna said.

But Jaclyn shook her head. "It seems simple enough to me. I saw you in that coffee shop, remember? I knew then that it was the job for you. You were in the right place at the right time. Sometimes things are just meant to be. You just need to trust that this is one of them and give it your all."

Anna was still unsure, and a little terrified, but Jaclyn's words were oddly calming. She seemed so sure that Anna started to feel a bit more confident, too. Maybe she could do this, or at least try. It wasn't like she had any other options.

"Thanks, Jaclyn. I really do appreciate it. I think I have the new job jitters."

"I know. You'll be just fine, though."

Patty, their waitress, came over and took their dinner order. The restaurant ran a buy-one, get-one free pizza special on trivia night, so they ordered their usual selection and once she left to put their order in, Jaclyn leaned forward with a twinkle in her eye.

As soon as she had everyone's attention, she spoke. "Wade Weston, what's this rumor I'm hearing about film people coming to the ranch? Are they just taking a vacation or is something happening that I need to know?"

Anna looked Tammy's way, and she shrugged. Anna wondered what on earth Jaclyn was talking about? She did notice Bernie and Lily exchange glances, though, and they both worked for Wade. So, maybe there was something interesting going on.

Wade laughed. "You don't miss much, Jaclyn, do you? It's true. There is something going on. We're keeping it quiet still so word doesn't get out too soon, but I can tell you all and it's pretty exciting news, I think. A pilot is going to be filmed here on the ranch and if it gets picked up, a TV series will film here. So you may see some construction going on for sets and some vehicles coming and going. You might even recognize some famous faces."

"Oooh, that is exciting. Can you say who?"

"Not yet. I don't know until it's all finalized. But we'll know soon."

"Do you suppose there would ever be a need for an older woman, say around my age, for any of their scenes. What do they call it, extras?"

"You know, there might be. I can find out and let you know. I'm assuming you're interested for yourself?"

Jaclyn smiled. "I might very well be. It sounds like fun."

"Would you want to be an extra?" Anna asked Tammy, and she shuddered at the thought.

"No, thanks. I prefer to be behind the camera, not in front of it." Tammy did take great pictures.

"I feel the same way. It will be fun to watch, though."

"Maybe I should look into being an extra, too,"

Clark said. "I've always thought it would be fun to be an actor."

Tammy laughed. "You are a bit of a ham. I can totally see you doing that."

She turned her attention back to Anna and asked, "So, how did the evil step monster react when you told her you're moving in with America's most eligible billionaire bachelor, as his nanny?"

"I didn't tell her. I don't trust her not to try to ruin it. Especially if she finds out I'm his nanny, of all things."

Tammy sighed. "I know. I don't blame you for keeping quiet. But weren't you tempted?"

Anna grinned. "Of course I was!"

ANNA PACKED up her room when she got home from trivia. She managed to fit everything she owned into three large suitcases and a few boxes. She started to cry again when she got to the three framed pictures of her father. Even though she'd had years to prepare for it and accept his death, it was still so hard. She thought she was handling it well, but now and then she'd see something that reminded her of him and the tears would come.

Her mother had died when she was very little so she didn't remember her the way she would have liked. Her father had stayed single for a long time, until about ten years ago, when Anna was thirteen and in eighth grade. That's when Anna's life changed again, and not for the better.

She hadn't realized how lonely her father must have been. It was the two of them for as long as she could remember until Elise came along. But, to her credit, Anna knew that she made her father happy. He only saw the good in Elise and was blind to her faults. Elise never showed her true colors around her father, either. She saved them for Anna and made it clear once she had children that the four of them were her family and Anna was the outsider.

She sighed as she carefully wrapped the pictures with some of her clothes so they wouldn't be damaged. Her plan was to leave in the morning as soon as Elise was gone and to just leave a note letting her know she was out of her hair. She was not going to leave a forwarding address. If Elise needed to reach her—and Anna couldn't imagine why she would—she had her cell phone number.

The next morning, she got up and had breakfast as if it was just another day. She wished Elise well as she left for work and as soon as she was out the door, Anna wrote her a note asking her to say goodbye to Tommy and Hayley. She felt bad not saying goodbye to them in person, but they were away visiting their grandparents for the week and besides, she thought Elise could best explain why she was no longer living there.

She plugged Ben's address in her Honda Civic's

GPS and drove off. Twenty minutes later, she reached the driveway to the ranch. It was a long, winding road that finally brought her to the main house—which took her breath away. It had sounded nice when Ben described it but it was truly beautiful. She wasn't exactly sure where to park but saw a four-car garage just past the house and parked in front of it. She grabbed her purse and her smallest suitcase, a carryon that had wheels. She could come back for the rest once she was situated and knew which room was hers.

She made her way to the front door and it was opened by a roly-poly woman with gray hair and a welcoming smile. She was wearing an apron over her flowered top and black pants.

"You must be Anna!"

"I am, yes."

"I'm Mrs. Higgins. But you can call me Betty. Come on in. I'll show you to your room so you can put that bag down, then I'll give you the tour. Ben's in the shower, but should be down shortly and he'll bring in your bags and put your car in the garage. You'll use the one on the far right. I have the one on the left and Ben uses the two in the middle," she explained.

Anna followed her to the second level, and down a long hallway to a guest bedroom that was spacious and had beautiful views of the mountains. The walls were a soft blue-gray shade, and the floors were polished hard wood with a plush cream carpet that filled most of the room. Anna's shoes sank into it as she walked. The bed was a queen size and had a fluffy white comforter topped with an assortment of throw pillows in various shades of blue and gray. It was a peaceful, restful room and Anna was looking forward to a good night's sleep later.

"Across the hall is Taylor's room. We thought it was best for you to be near her. Ben's room is next to Taylor's and at the other end of the house, there are two more guest bedrooms."

"Do you live-in, too?" Anna was curious where Betty's room was.

"I do, but I'm in the smaller cottage you may have noticed as you pulled in the driveway. It's just before the main house. It's quite lovely and perfect for me."

Betty showed her the rest of the house—the cozy office/den, formal living room, comfortable family room, dining room, finished basement with a pool table and theater area. She finished the tour in the kitchen, which looked like a professional chef's dream kitchen with its all white cabinets, six-burner gas stove, double ovens, and oversized island with a stunning white marble countertop.

"Have a seat. Ben should be down any minute. I'm going to have a second cup of coffee. Would you like one?"

"Sure. Thank you." Anna settled onto one of the chairs around the island and once she had coffee for both of them, Betty joined her.

"Have you worked here long?" Anna asked her.

"Almost six weeks. Ben hired me as soon as he got here. I do everything for him. Mostly cleaning and cooking and making sure he eats. He's one of those people who gets so busy that he often skips one, sometimes even two meals."

Anna laughed. "I don't think I've ever skipped a meal in my life!"

"You and me both. I'm usually thinking ahead to what I'll eat next." She patted her stomach. "Sometimes that gets me in trouble."

"Where is Taylor?" Anna noticed that it was unusually quiet.

"She's sleeping. Ben gave her a bottle before he got in the shower. She'll probably be down for at least an hour or two. He's gotten pretty good at managing his schedule around her naps. But it doesn't always work. Babies have their own unpredictable schedules."

Almost on cue, Anna heard a plaintive cry.

"Speaking of unpredictable. Poor baby. She's teething."

The cries grow louder and a moment later, Ben walked into the kitchen carrying the baby carrier. He set it on the island, not far from the edge and Anna froze for a moment as a wave of fear washed over her. She took a deep breath and then stepped forward and pushed the carrier further into the middle of the island and away from the edge.

"Sorry. I can be clumsy and having that too close to the edge makes me nervous."

"Thanks. I love that you thought to do that. Maybe you can work your magic again with her." Ben picked Taylor up, gave her a quick cuddle and then handed her to Anna. The tiny girl's face looked up at hers and at the sight of her sweet, trusting eyes, her heart melted. She put her finger out and the baby grabbed it in her hand and squeezed tight. She cuddled her close and patted her back until she burped several times and then fell asleep again. When she was sure she was totally out, she carefully set her in her bed and looked up to see both Betty and Ben watching her with pleased expressions.

"See, I told you I found a good one," Ben said to Betty.

"You did say that. I would tend to agree. Now, shall we all enjoy our coffee?"

Anna settled back into her seat and Betty added a splash of hot coffee to her mug.

"Betty showed you around?"

Anna nodded. "She did. Your house is lovely."

He smiled. "Thank you. It is peaceful here. I worried that it might be too quiet but I'm loving it. There's no one distracting me—except for Taylor, of course—but she's different. And with technology, I can work from anywhere. The wifi is surprisingly good here."

"He lives on his computer." Betty shook her head.

Ben laughed. "I do, actually. In fact, I'm going to head into the office in a minute, and I'll be tied up on calls and online meetings for most of the day. But, don't hesitate to interrupt me if you need something. I'll probably skip lunch unless Betty sneaks a sandwich in and I remember to eat it. But, I'll probably see you back here for dinner."

Anna nodded. She liked the idea of having the day to herself to get used to the place and for Taylor to get used to her.

"I'll go grab your bags in a minute, too, and bring them up to your room. Oh, there's one more thing." He got up and disappeared into his office for a moment, then came back and handed a slim box to Anna. It was a brand new MacAir laptop. Anna had a laptop, but it was a very old and painfully slow generic windows one.

"What's this for?"

Ben grinned. "The main office sent me a bunch of files and office supplies that I'd ordered and somehow they sent two new laptops instead of one. It's easier to just give it to you than to send it back. So, enjoy! Oh, wifi password is Rivers End Ranch. Thought that would be easy to remember."

A moment later, he was gone, and it was like all the energy left the room. Betty looked at her and smiled, and Anna got the feeling she was reading her mind when she said, "Feels quiet in here now, huh? That's Ben. He's like one of those Energizer bunnies, just goes and goes until he drops."

CHAPTER 3

Ben brought Anna's bags up to her room then grabbed a breakfast bar, topped off his coffee and disappeared into his office. As he turned on his computer, he tried not to think of how cute Anna had looked. She was even prettier than he'd remembered, with her long, pale blond hair. It fell to her shoulders and was sleek and straight. Her jeans were well worn and fit her slim figure perfectly. He also liked her floaty, peach-colored top and caramel-colored cowboy boots. They were a different pair than the ones he'd seen her in before at the coffee shop. He made a note of the fact that she liked cowboy boots. He did that when he met people, filed away little mental notes about things that stuck out about them. It was helpful when the holidays rolled around. He'd once remembered that his sister liked red sweaters. Except he wouldn't be buying her any more sweaters.

He stared out the window and thought about his sister for a moment. They'd always been close and losing her had been one of the hardest things he'd ever gone through. He couldn't even imagine how hard it must have been for his parents. They had all lived in the Silicon Valley area, but after Jessica died, his parents decided to sell their house and move to Florida. It was something they'd always talked about doing and with Jessica gone and Ben deciding to move, there was no reason for them not to go, too. He'd tried to talk them into coming to Riston, but Florida in the winter had always been their dream. They did promise to come for a long visit during the hot summer months, though.

He never knew what might trigger thoughts of Jessica. Sometimes it was a song, or a picture or a date, like her birthday or holiday. Christmas had been especially hard this year. And now he had her baby. His parents had offered to take Taylor, but he wouldn't hear of it. He and Jessica had talked about the possibility of this day coming, though they'd both been thinking more along the lines of a freak accident or something, not cancer. But he'd agreed—insisted, actually—to take Taylor and raise her as his own. And he didn't think of Taylor as his niece. He did at first, but after just a few weeks, they'd bonded and now she was his daughter. Jessica had never married so they shared the same last name, but if they hadn't he would have adopted her so that they did.

As much as he loved that little girl, he was relieved that Anna was there to help. This way, he'd be able to make sure that any time he had with Taylor was quality time, when he could focus his attention on her totally. He had a new respect for single parents. For all parents, actually. Being a parent was hard work.

He smiled as he thought back to how chaotic his first weeks with Taylor had been when he was naïve enough to think he could juggle feeding her and being on a conference call at the same time. He'd screwed up repeatedly, but he learned quickly and now he could change a diaper as well as anyone. His phone rang and brought his thoughts back to the present. It was time for his first conference call.

His morning flew until it was almost noon and time for him to head over to River's End Ranch for a meeting with Wade. They were going to have lunch at Kelsey's Kafe and Wade wanted to introduce him to Steven. The name was familiar and when Wade explained who he was it made sense. He'd asked his friend, Adiel, about him and he said they'd worked together once on a project and it had been a good experience. Given that information, Ben was intrigued to find out what Wade had in mind.

When Ben arrived at Wade's office, he smiled at the chaos he seemed to walk into. Bernie, Wade's assistant, was on the phone while a FedEx delivery guy stood waiting for a signature. The other girl, Lily, had a mother and what he guessed were her four daughters gathered around a portfolio with pictures of wedding cakes. Meanwhile, her phone was ringing off the hook and she was letting it go to voicemail so she could give her full attention to the people in front of her. Ben approved of that whole-heartedly. Not that it mattered, of course, but one of his pet peeves was someone leaving the customers they were helping in person to attend to someone calling on the phone.

Since both girls were more than busy, Ben poked his head into Wade's office. He was on a call but waved Ben in and gestured for him to have a seat. A moment later, he hung up the phone. It immediately rang again. Wade glanced at it, scowled and stood up. "Let's go. Whoever that is can leave a voice message."

Ben followed him outside and when they stepped on the front porch, Wade pulled something out of his pocket and clicked it. He heard a whirring sound and then was impressed to see a golf cart back itself up, turn around and head their way. It pulled up right in front of them, and Wade looked delighted.

"What do you think? Cool trick, huh? A vendor dropped this off last week for me to try it out. He wants me to fall in love with it and buy a few more."

"Think you will?"

"Probably," Wade admitted. "Why not? I bet the guests will love it!"

Ben agreed and was tempted to order one himself.

"Hop in. We could walk. But it's kind of a hike and I'd rather spend the time at lunch. Steven and his business partner Brandon Chin, should be there waiting for us. Brandon is the one that finds most of their investors and sponsors."

"So, are you going to tell me what this is all about?" Ben asked.

Wade chuckled. "Honestly, I don't know much more than what I told you already. Steven is executive producer for a TV project that will be filming here at the ranch. He mentioned that they were still looking for some additional investors and asked me if I knew you."

"Okay, good enough. I asked my friend Adiel about him. Turns out they've worked together and he gave him the thumb's up. I look forward to hearing what he has to say."

"Have you been to Kelsey's Kafe yet? My sister manages it and the food is pretty amazing. It's stick-to-your-ribs kind of stuff. Bob makes a burger so good it will make you cry. Though you can't go wrong with one of his specials, either."

When they walked through the door, a pretty blonde woman ran over to them and gave Wade a big hug. She glanced at the clock on the wall. "You're actually early. Did you take the golf cart?"

"We did."

"I want one. All of us do. We can discuss at Sunday dinner. But the consensus is the more of these golf carts at the ranch the better. Remotes for everyone! Oh, Steven and another man are already here, waiting for you in the corner booth. Root beer?"

Wade nodded and Kelsi looked his way.

"And what about you? Root beer okay or do you want something else?"

"That's fine for me, too."

"Good. Oh, by the way, I'm Kelsi. This rude one's sister."

Wade smiled and apologized. "I'm sorry, I should have introduced you. Kelsi, this is Ben Turner. He recently moved here."

Kelsi nodded and ran off to get their drinks. Ben couldn't help but notice that she and Wade shared the same icy blue eyes that were almost startling, they were so light.

Wade shook his head. "My sister is always feisty, but she's been unusually so lately."

"She seems great."

"Oh, I'm not complaining. There's never a dull moment with Kelsi."

Wade introduced Ben and Steven introduced Brandon to both of them and they sat across from him in the booth. Ben noticed that Brandon was still wearing his coat even though they were inside.

"He's not used to cold weather here," Steven said with a laugh.

Kelsi returned a moment later with their drinks and menus.

"Bob's special today is shepherd's pie. There's also

a low-fat version in case that interests you. I'll be back in a few minutes." Kelsi dropped the menus on the table and Ben smiled. She'd made it abundantly clear that she was not a fan of diet versions. He had to agree. He'd rather hit the gym or have less of the real thing than a low-fat imitation.

When she came back for their orders, they all got the full-fat special. Kelsi nodded in approval and took their menus away.

"So, I filled Ben in with what I know about your project," Wade said.

Steven smiled. "I was surprised and delighted to learn you moved to Riston. Is this a permanent move? Or more of a short-term thing? Just curious."

"I hope it will be permanent. I needed to get out of the public eye, now that it's not just me I have to worry about."

"I heard about your niece and the passing of your sister. I'm very sorry."

Ben appreciated that. "Thank you."

"I read that you stepped down as CEO of Blue Sky Pages and wasn't sure, given your move, if you were planning to continue investing in film and TV projects?"

Ben nodded. "I stepped down because it was time. The company doesn't need me there on a daily basis anymore. I'm still a majority shareholder and very involved, but more on an advisory basis. Which frees up more time for various investment projects."

"That's encouraging to hear."

Ben grinned. "And I don't have to be present in LA, either, to invest in these types of projects. Now that people know what I've done, they don't seem to have any problem reaching me by email."

Steven nodded. "Good. But I have to admit, I'm excited that you are local as we'd love your input if what we are doing interests you."

"That is definitely a selling point. Even though the bulk of what I do can be done remotely now, I still always visit the set of any production I invest in just to take the pulse of what's going on and to weigh in if I have any insight to offer."

"Great. So, let me fill you in on what we're doing..."

For the next forty-five minutes, Steven went into great detail about the project and the book that it was based on. They only paused briefly when Kelsi delivered their meals. The conversation continued over dessert and coffee.

"The only thing we haven't nailed down yet is the head writer/show runner position. We have a few people in mind, but the challenge is they are all involved in other projects. So, it's a matter of timing."

Ben sipped his coffee, and a thought occurred to him. He was ninety-five percent sure that he wanted to get involved. The project sounded great, and he loved that it was local. That would satisfy his need for occasional people interaction.

"So, what do you think?" Steven finally asked as Kelsi set the check on the table.

"I'm interested. I'll have to do my due diligence, of course, and check out the book this is based on and the list of people who have committed so far."

Steven nodded, reached for something on the seat next to him and handed a paperback book to Ben.

"Here you go. I anticipated that you'd want a copy."

"Thanks. I have another thought, too. A suggestion that would make me more inclined to move forward if it worked out."

"What's that?" Steven looked excited and apprehensive at the same time.

"I understand you worked with a friend of mine before, Adiel Bozeman."

Steven smiled. "I know Adiel. He was great to work with."

"Would you consider him for your show runner? I asked him about you before I agreed to this meeting and he happened to mention that his current project is winding down."

"Adiel might be available? Yes, I'd certainly be interested in talking to him about this."

"Great, give him a call. And let's touch base after the two of you connect. I should be ready to make a decision by then."

. . .

ANNA WAS EXHAUSTED by the end of her first day watching Taylor. Who would have thought that minding an eleven-month-old baby would be so all-consuming? When she wasn't napping, Anna was getting ready for her to wake up, making sure she had her bottles of formula filled and cutting up finger food snacks for her—pieces of fruit, oatmeal, crackers. She was a good eater, not fussy at all, except when it seemed like her teeth were hurting.

While Betty bustled around the house, getting it in order, and Taylor napped, Anna fired up her new laptop and researched everything she needed to know to be a good nanny. One of the first things she did was to put the teething gel away, in a bathroom drawer. She'd read that the anesthetic was potentially unsafe for babies and a better alternative was a cold teething ring. She found several good candidates among Taylor's pacifiers and toys and after a thorough wash, filled them with water and put them in the freezer to chill.

By the time she fed Taylor dinner, changed her diaper, read a book to her and settled her down for the night, she returned to the kitchen where the lasagna Betty had put in the oven earlier was starting to smell amazing. Betty was making a shopping list and smiled when she saw Anna.

"There you are. I'm getting ready to head out for the night. The lasagna is ready to eat any time, so just help yourself. Ben usually surfaces from his office around six if you'd rather have some company."

"You don't stay for dinner?" Anna felt slightly alarmed at the thought of it just being her and Ben for the evening.

"No. I have a kitchen in my cottage and I'm not a big eater at dinner time. Tonight is bridge night with my girlfriends, so I'll be eating there. Unless there's anything you want me to pick up at the store tomorrow, I'll be off."

"I can't think of anything. Have a good night."

Betty smiled. "I hope your first day went well? I think it's going to be good having you here."

The comment took Anna by surprise. "Oh, thank you!"

When Betty left, the house felt oddly quiet. Taylor was sound asleep and the only sound was Anna's stomach as it grumbled so loudly she wouldn't have been surprised if Ben could hear it from his office. She smiled at the silly thought. She was starving, but didn't want to be rude and start eating if she was supposed to wait for him. They hadn't discussed mealtimes other than the fact that room and board was included in the position. She poured herself a glass of water and found some celery stalks to munch on while she waited. She didn't have to wait long. Just as she swallowed her last bite of celery, she heard footsteps coming down the hall.

"Are you as hungry as I am?" Ben asked as he walked into the kitchen.

"I could eat," Anna said casually as her stomach rumbled again.

Ben raised his eyebrows. "I'm sorry to keep you waiting. I should have mentioned before that you don't have to wait for me. If you're hungry and I'm not around, please go ahead." He grinned. "I am glad for the company, though. Shall I plate you up some lasagna? Betty has this on the regular rotation because I love it."

"Yes, please. I'll get the salad out." Anna set the large bowl of salad and the homemade Italian dressing Betty had made earlier on the island.

"We can eat right here, unless you'd rather go to the table?" Ben said. Anna followed his glance toward the formal dining room table.

"No, this is fine."

He handed her a plate with a large, oozing slab of lasagna and a buttery piece of garlic bread. He set his full plate next to hers and was about to sit down, then turned back to her with a question.

"How about some wine? I like a glass sometimes with dinner. Since today's your first day, and you're still here, I'd say we should toast to that."

"I'd love a glass of wine."

Ben poured them each some wine, then joined her at the island and helped himself to the salad.

Anna took a small bite of the lasagna and it was delicious. Betty was a good cook. Too good.

"Did you mention something about a workout room? If all of Betty's meals are this good, I could be in trouble."

Ben laughed. "I did. And they are. It's a small room, above the garage. There's a treadmill and elliptical machine, some weights. Nothing fancy, but enough to counteract Betty's food."

"I'll have to check that out soon, then."

Ben glanced at her and Anna felt a warm flush. She looked down and focused on her food.

"I think you're safe for a while. You're tiny."

Anna smiled. She wasn't anything close to tiny, but it was still nice to hear it. She knew she wasn't overweight, but it was because she was careful. She had to be. She loved food, and it was easy to lose control. She had quickly gained and then slowly lost fifteen pounds her first year in college. The freshman fifteen was a very real thing.

"Thank you."

"So, how was your first day? I hope it wasn't too boring for you?" He looked a little worried and Anna reassured him she wasn't going anywhere. The job had come along at just the right time and she was grateful for it.

"It was good. I didn't have time to be bored. I was surprised by how fast the time went. How was your day?" She was curious about what he did.

"It was busy. I had a meeting at River's End Ranch. A lunch meeting, actually, at Kelsey's Kafe. Have you been there?"

"Yes. I always liked it there, but since the new chef came, the food is amazing. Bob knows comfort food."

Ben laughed. "Yes. He does. It was a good place for a business lunch. Did you know they are going to be filming a TV show at the ranch?"

"I heard something about that at trivia the other night."

"Trivia?"

"Every Thursday night they do team trivia at the restaurant at the ranch. A bunch of us play often. Wade told us about it the other night. Well, after Jaclyn asked him that is. She'd already heard some rumors."

"Who is this Jaclyn? I've heard her name a few times now."

Anna told him all about Jaclyn, though she left out her match-making tendencies. He wouldn't care about that.

"She sounds like quite a character."

"She is. So, why did they want to talk to you about the TV project?" Anna asked.

"They're looking for a few more investors and it's right up my alley."

"Are you going to do it?" It sounded exciting to Anna.

"I think so. But I haven't committed yet. I'm hoping

they will hire a friend of mine on as show runner. If they do, that will make the project a lot more fun and I'll probably be over there more often."

"Well, I hope it works out for you. I've read that book, the one they are basing the TV series on, and it's awesome. I read it in one sitting."

"Really? Is that normal for you?" Ben looked keenly interested in her answer.

"No. Not at all. I watch more movies than I read books, just because I love movies. For me to read a book in one sitting means the book hooked me instantly and I couldn't put it down. That rarely happens. But I guess it's why the book has gone on to be such a huge seller."

BEN TOOK another big bite of lasagna and thought about what Anna had said. He'd been pretty sure he wanted to get involved with the TV project but wanted to read the book first. Now he realized that he didn't need to. At least not before deciding. He'd still read it because that's what he did. He was thorough. But hearing that Anna, someone who wasn't a huge reader, couldn't put the book down, set all his alarms buzzing. It meant the book had huge commercial appeal, which was already evident since it was on the bestseller list. But still, hearing from an actual reader made a difference.

"I'm having another slice of lasagna. Do you want some?" He cut a big slice for himself and looked back at Anna to see if she wanted more, too.

"I really shouldn't," she said. But it was obvious that she wanted more.

"Give me your plate."

She handed it to him and he cut a smaller slice.

"Thank you."

Ben settled back into his seat and in minutes his plate was clean. Anna was still nibbling away at hers.

"So, tell me more about you. You got into law school, which is awesome. What's the issue with finances? Once you apply for financial aid, I bet you'll be surprised what is available."

Anna took a deep breath and Ben sensed that she was debating how much to share with him.

"It's not that easy. My step-mother informed me that I'm out of the will and she's not interested in helping me with any financial aid. She says that there's not much money left, and she admitted that she lied to my father and told him I got scholarships everywhere so I didn't need his money."

Ben didn't like the sound of that at all. "Didn't your father ask you about it?"

Anna shook her head sadly. "No. He was confused in the months before he passed. His cancer had spread to his brain, which messed with his memory and mobility. It was heartbreaking to see. So, I never talked to him about anything like that. I just focused on happy memories."

Ben nodded, thinking of his sister and her similar memory issues. He understood totally. But he was furious on Anna's behalf. Something sounded very fishy about her stepmother.

"Have you thought of fighting the will? I'd be happy to help."

Anna looked happy about the idea at first but then she shook her head.

"No. I don't want to go there. I just want to find another way, even if it takes me longer. I have my issues with Elise, but I love her children, Hayley and Tommy, and I don't want to cause any problems."

"Okay. Forget I said anything, then. I'm going to head back into my office for a while. Feel free to make yourself at home in the living room if you feel like watching TV."

Anna yawned. "Thanks. I think I'm going to just go relax in my room for a bit and head to bed. I'm not used to getting up this early," she admitted.

Ben laughed. "Welcome to my world. I'm glad you're here, Anna. Sweet dreams."

CHAPTER 4

When Anna got up the next day, she was surprised by how quiet the house was. She checked the time and it was almost eight o'clock. She'd expected Taylor to be awake and needing her attention by seven at the latest. She scrambled out of bed, pulled on jeans and a sweatshirt and poked her head in Taylor's bedroom. Her crib was empty.

Before she reached the kitchen, she heard low voices and the sound of a baby laughing. Betty was buttering toast while Ben was trying to feed what looked like peaches to Taylor, who kept spitting them out.

"I'm so sorry. I meant to be up earlier," she apologized.

But Ben just smiled. "No worries. I'm happy to have breakfast with my daughter."

Anna quickly got a soft cloth and cleaned up the peachy mess all over Taylor's face and the surrounding area. There was even a big glob of it in Ben's hair, but he didn't seem to notice.

"Do you want me to get that for you? It looks like she flung her food in your hair."

Ben ran a hand through his hair and got most of the peaches out of it.

"She sure did. I'll be jumping in the shower after this anyway, so it's all good."

"Do you want me to take over?" Anna asked.

"No, we're just about done. You could get her bottle ready, though, if you like."

Anna warmed up Taylor's bottle of formula and a few minutes later, Ben handed her to Anna. She got her situated with her bottle and didn't even notice at first that Ben was watching them with interest.

"You're very good with her. Did you used to baby sit a lot when you were younger? Before you started nannying?"

"Yes, I did. For a while." She shivered at the thought. If Ben knew the truth about what she'd done and why she stopped babysitting, he never would have hired her. She bit her lower lip, hoping that he'd never find out.

"Oh, why did you stop? Did you find something more glamorous?" he teased.

She took a deep breath and told him the truth— well, part of the truth. "I got a job working the concession stand at the local movie theater. Perks were free movies and all the popcorn I could eat."

"And you love movies..." he said with a smile. "Oh, I meant to mention this before, but you don't have to be stuck here all day. Feel free to take Taylor out and about with you. If you need to run errands or want to meet a friend for lunch."

"Are you sure?"

"Of course. I trust you." He leaned over and dropped a kiss on Taylor's forehead. "Okay, I'm off to the showers. Have a good day."

Anna watched him go and thought about his suggestion. She was excited and terrified at the thought of taking Taylor out. What if something happened?

Betty was looking at her curiously. "You really should get out for a while. It will be good for both of you. Taylor could use some fresh air and a change of scenery and I imagine you could, too. You don't want to be cooped up here all day long, every day."

"I'll think about it."

"Her carrier is in the front hall closet. It's a top of the line model, easy to snap right into your backseat. I can help you with it if you're not sure."

Anna smiled. "Thanks. If I get stuck, I'll come find you. Maybe we will go for a ride later. A friend of mine manages the book store at the ranch. They have a great selection of children's books and toys."

"That's a great idea. Taylor could use some new books. She loves being read to."

Anna texted Tammy, and they made plans to meet later that afternoon. She could bring Taylor to the store and then take a quick coffee break with Tammy at Sadie's Saloon.

Once both she and Taylor had eaten lunch, Anna went and found a stroller and baby carrier in the front hall closet and carefully secured first the base and then the carrier in her car's back seat. Once she was confident that she had it set up correctly, and she'd tested clicking the carrier into it and removing it several times, she brought the carrier back into the house and gently placed Taylor into it. She tucked a soft fleece blanket around her and handed her her favorite plush stuffed animal. Anna smiled at the sight of the funny looking toy. It was a miniature Bigfoot, which she'd thought was hysterical when she first saw it.

"Seems an odd choice for a baby," she'd commented to Betty, who laughed in response.

"I couldn't agree more. It caught Ben's eye at the gift shop at River's End Ranch when he first moved here. Apparently Kelsi, one of the Weston siblings that owns the ranch, is obsessed with finding Bigfoot. Ben said there's all kinds of Bigfoot paraphernalia in the shop—toys, books, t-shirts, sweatshirts, even pool towels all with the image of Bigfoot on it. He thought it was funny. Joke was on him, though, when it turned out to be Taylor's favorite toy."

Anna glanced at Taylor, who was happily sucking

on one of Bigfoot's ears. It was obvious by the worn and faded spots that Bigfoot was well loved.

"Okay, I think we're off. Maybe I'll find a picture book on Bigfoot for her!"

"Have fun," Betty said as she opened the front door for them.

———————

TAMMY WAS at the cash register, ringing up a customer, when Anna wheeled Taylor's stroller into the bookstore. Tammy waved when she saw them and Anna went to the children's section. She'd been in the bookstore a few times before but hadn't had a reason to check out the children's books. She was impressed by the selection. She recognized a lot of old favorites like Dr. Seuss and some cute newer ones like the Fancy Nancy picture books and one that made her smile, Dragons Love Tacos.

She picked out a few cute ones with just a few words per page and lots of fun pictures and brought them to the counter. Tammy rang them up and approved her choices.

"She'll love these." As she put them in a bag and handed Anna her receipt, a woman came out of an office in the back. Tammy introduced her as Melissa, the owner of the store.

"Nice to meet you. Enjoy your coffee break."

"Do you want me to bring you a mocha?" Tammy offered.

"I don't really need it, but yes, I'd love that. Extra whipped cream, please."

"Of course!"

"She seems really nice," Anna said as they headed toward Sadie's Saloon, which was just a short walk.

"Melissa's great. And she's a really good writer, too. I just read her second mystery and I couldn't put it down."

"Oh, maybe I should have bought a copy. I want to start reading more."

"You can borrow mine when I'm done."

"Oh, thanks. I'm surprised you didn't get the ebook version."

"Normally I do. But if it's author I love, sometimes I'll get the print copy. Especially when it's someone I know and they autograph it."

"That makes sense."

The coffee shop was busier than the last time they'd been there. The owner of the shop, Sadie, was chatting with the customers in front of them, and handing out tiny plastic spoons with ice cream samples.

"Oh, Sadie must have a new flavor out today," Tammy said as the people in front of them paid and then it was their turn.

"Hi, Tammy. Would you and your friend like to try a new flavor I'm experimenting with?" Sadie said.

They both said yes at the same time and laughed.

"Here you go." Sadie handed them both a bite of ice cream. "It's peanut butter with caramel swirl and bits of chocolate. What do you think?"

"I think I need a cup of that, and a coffee," Tammy said. She looked back at Anna. "How about you?"

"I wasn't planning on getting ice cream, but I can't sit there and watch you eat it," Anna laughed. "I'll have the same."

They brought their coffees and ice creams over to a table and sat down. Anna pulled Taylor's stroller close to the table so it wouldn't be in the way. Taylor was wide awake and looking all around the room with big, curious eyes.

"She's super cute! How is everything going?" Tammy asked.

"She is, isn't she? So far, so good. Though I was a nervous wreck at first about taking her out. I put the carrier in the back seat several times before I was sure that it was locked into place."

Tammy looked sympathetic. "It wasn't your fault, you know. If anything, it was Elise's."

Anna was silent for a moment and then nodded. "I know. Rationally, I know that, but I still feel guilty. And it doesn't help that Elise still blames me for it."

Tammy's eyes narrowed at the mention of Elise. There was no love lost there.

"Well, it's never been fair. You know how I feel about it. And besides, he's fine now. No harm done."

"Right. So, how's your day going?" Anna tried to change the subject. She appreciated that Tammy got fired up on her behalf, but she still preferred to not even think about it.

"Good. That cute doctor I met the other night at trivia came into the store today."

"Clark? The one that was sitting next to you?"

"That's the one. He's a huge flirt, so it's hard to tell if he might be interested or if he's just charming to everyone. I'm pretty sure it's not just me."

Anna looked at her friend. Tammy was gorgeous. She was taller than Anna, and had brown hair that was so dark it almost looked black and it fell half-way down her back, shiny and straight. And she had unusual, bluish gray eyes and pale skin. The combination was striking. Tammy had always gotten more attention from boys than Anna did, but she didn't mind.

"It probably was you. Did he buy anything?"

"The newest Lee Child thriller and a couple of crossword puzzle books."

"He likes crossword puzzles?"

"He said they help him to relax and unwind after a long day."

"So, he has a somewhat serious side, then. Did he ask you out?"

Tammy laughed. "No. Though he did ask if I was going to be at trivia this week."

"So he came into your shop and asked if you'd be at trivia? Could be a little interest there, maybe."

"I'm sure he was just being friendly. And he's good friends with Wade so probably stopped by to see him before coming to the store. I highly doubt it was just to see me."

"Right."

"So, what about your billionaire? Tell me more about Ben. Aside from being insanely good-looking, is he nice?"

"He is, actually. Nicer than I expected." She told Tammy about waking up to find Ben already up and feeding Taylor.

"And it was his idea for you to come here today?"

"Well, not specifically here, but to get out of the house."

"He sounds great. Is he single?"

Was he? It seemed as though he probably was, but Anna realized she didn't know much about Ben's personal life. Maybe he had a long-distance relationship with someone.

"I think so, but I'm not really sure."

"I remember reading about him in the tabloids. Always a different girl, usually someone famous. But now that I think about it, I haven't seen any mentions on him or any women in a long time."

"He said that was a reason he moved here. To get out of the spotlight and focus on raising Taylor in a more normal environment."

"Well, once the women in Riston catch wind that

he's here, that's likely to change. He's the most eligible bachelor this town has ever seen."

"I suppose so." For some reason, Anna found the thought of Ben dating anyone in Riston a bit depressing.

"Maybe it will be you," Tammy said with a slightly teasing tone, but Anna could tell there was a little hope there, too.

"It's not like that. I work for him and I need this job. I wouldn't do anything that could jeopardize it."

Tammy nodded. "I understand. So, fill me in on the school situation. Have you looked into what you need to do for financial aid?"

Anna took a sip of her coffee before answering. "I have and what I found out isn't good. In order to qualify for financial aid, I need Elise to fill out some forms and she made it clear she wants nothing to do with helping me go to law school. Besides, even if she did, it wouldn't matter because I still wouldn't qualify."

Tammy looked confused. "Why not? I thought you said she said there wasn't a lot of money left when your father passed."

"She lied. He may have lost some, but last I knew he had all of his money in one stock—Amazon, and that's done nothing but go up in recent years. So even if it did fall, and it is a volatile stock, even with a dip, he should still be somewhat ahead. Enough for me not to qualify for aid."

"I'm sorry. That really stinks. What will you do?"

That was the big question. Law school was expensive and even if she saved every penny she made, she still wouldn't have enough to cover tuition and room and board by September.

"I don't know. I'll need to see what I can do for loans, and how much I can save. I might need to push it off a year."

Anna took her last bite of ice cream just as Taylor decided it was time to go. She let out a huge holler and then the tears came.

"I think she's ready to head home," Anna said as she stood and looked around for where to throw out her trash.

"I'll take those," Tammy said. "I'm going to order Melissa's mocha and then we can be on our way."

BEN STARED out his office window, taking in a sight he'd never seen in Silicon Valley. About a hundred yards from the house, in a pretty meadow, six deer were roaming around, stopping occasionally to nibble on some grass. He'd been glued to his computer screen all day, so the short break and peaceful sight was a welcome one. He stretched and twisted in his chair to loosen up his crunchy muscles. He'd have to visit his gym later and get a good workout in. That helped keep him in shape and get a good night's sleep. It would also take his mind off his pretty new nanny who was sleeping just down the hall. He'd been so desperate to find someone capable to watch Taylor that it hadn't even occurred to him that a young, pretty nanny could be a dangerous distraction.

Ben liked dating all kinds of women. Admittedly, he'd done his share of it, and it had been fun walking the red carpet with actresses and models and other lovely women he'd met. As a well-known billionaire, he hadn't ever had a shortage of women interested in going out with him. But, he'd always kept things light. His number one focus had always been on his job and he made it clear with everyone he dated that he wasn't looking for anything serious. Most of them felt the same way, but he knew a few of them thought they'd be able to change his mind and saw it as a challenge. He also knew most were as attracted to his money as they were to him.

And after a while, he'd grown tired of it. Eventually, he hoped to meet someone that he could be serious with. His priorities had changed now that he had Taylor to consider and truthfully, going out with different women all the time got old after a while. But, while he hoped to eventually meet someone in Riston, he knew that the last candidate he should consider would be his live-in nanny. That just seemed like a recipe for disaster. If it didn't go well, he'd be out of a nanny for one thing. No, he'd just have to resist the temptation to flirt with her, and focus on keeping his distance and just being her friend. Plus, he had to admit, she hadn't shown the slightest interest in him other than as an employer. Maybe he was losing his touch.

His phone rang, and he smiled when he saw who it was—Adiel.

"So, what did you think? Did you talk to Steven yet?" Ben asked

"I did. Thank you for the head's up. It sounds right up my alley and it would be fun to hang out in Riston with you for a few months, or maybe longer if the pilot gets picked up."

"Did you say yes, then?"

"Steven's sending over the contract now, and I'm flying in on Sunday to drop it off in person and walk around the property with him. Get a feel for his vision."

Ben was thrilled to hear it. Except for his friend Jack who worked for the local police and had recently married, Ben didn't have any close friends in Riston, and it would be fun to have someone to hang out with.

"I couldn't be happier to hear this. You're welcome to crash here. I've got plenty of room," Ben offered.

"I will gladly take you up on that for a night or two. I'll just be in town for a few days, then back in a week or so to stay. Steven said there will be some housing set up for everyone working on the show. It will either be right on the ranch or close by. I'm not sure on the details yet."

"Well, I'm looking forward to catching up when you get here. Congrats."

"Thanks again for putting my name forward. I really appreciate it. I'll see you in a few days."

BEN GLANCED out the window again as he hung up the phone. The deer were long gone. But the view was still breathtaking. There were snow-capped mountains in the distance, soaring green trees and glistening lakes. Riston was beautiful and something about the air here really agreed with him. Just looking out the window at the serene views filled him with a sense of peace, and the sureness that this was where he was meant to be.

CHAPTER 5

When Anna pulled in the driveway, she smiled at the sight of a half-dozen or so deer grazing in the backyard. Growing up in Riston, it was a sight she was used to but never got sick of. As she was getting Taylor and her carrier out of the backseat, she thought she saw movement in one of the windows, in the room that Ben used as an office.

When she came into the house, Ben's door was closed and she could faintly hear him talking on the phone. Betty came over to help and shut the door behind them. Taylor was ready for a diaper change and a bottle, in that order, and when she brought her to the kitchen for the bottle, she caught a whiff of whatever Betty was stirring on the stove.

"It's chicken stew for your dinner tonight and I just took a loaf of bread out of the oven."

So, that was what smelled so good. Fresh baked bread. She would definitely need to check out that gym soon.

"Yum."

"There's some leftover lasagna, too. I figured you might want to have that for lunch tomorrow. Ben made a good dent in it today."

"You're going to fatten me up," Anna said with a smile.

"If I do, then I consider it a job well done. Want to try a piece of the bread? I was just about to have a slice with a cup of tea. You can keep me company."

"Okay, twist my arm," Anna said as Betty slid a plate with a thick slice of buttered bread across the island. Taylor's started making noises when she saw Anna eating the bread and she broke off a small piece and gave it to her.

"Taylor likes it."

Anna spent an enjoyable hour chatting with Betty and feeding bits of bread and butter to Taylor. She learned that both of her children were married. Her son Philip was a resident at Mass General Hospital in Boston and her daughter, Andrea, was a corporate lawyer for a top firm in New York City.

"They're both doing wonderfully with their careers and are too busy to have children. I keep asking and they tell me as soon as things slow down, then maybe. I'm not holding my breath that it will be any time soon."

"Do you think either of them might ever move back home, to Riston?"

Betty's eyes clouded a bit. "I'd love that, of course, but it doesn't seem likely for either of them. But, you never do know what the future holds." She cut another slice of bread and gave most of it to Taylor. "At least I have this little one to entertain me," she said with a smile.

The clock on the wall chimed that it was five o'clock, time for Betty to head home.

"Any fun plans tonight?" Anna asked her.

"Yes. I'm heading to my sister Josephine's house for dinner. She lives just down the road. It is nice to have family nearby even if it's not my kids."

When Betty left, Anna scooped up Taylor and brought her into the living room to read to her for a while. She got a little fussy, but the cool teething ring seemed to help. She read to her until her eyes got heavy. She'd just closed one of the new books she'd bought that day when Ben walked into the room and saw the two of them on the sofa with picture books strewn about and Taylor dozing.

"Busy day? Looks like you did some shopping. I'll reimburse you for the books."

"Oh, you don't have to. I was just at the book store and picked a few up. She likes it when I read to her."

"Of course I will. I'll add it into your check. I appreciate it. I'd been meaning to get some more books for her. I think I've worn out Goodnight Moon."

Anna smiled. "She does like that one."

"Are you hungry? I was just going to have some dinner."

"Sure. I think Taylor will be out for a little while."

"Leave her here. She'll be fine while we eat. If she wakes up, she'll let us know."

Anna followed him into the kitchen. The layout of the house was open concept, so she could still see the living room sofa from where she sat at the island. If Taylor stirred, she could go get her.

Ben set two big bowls of soup and the loaf of bread and butter on the island. Anna cut herself a slice and buttered it generously.

"Did you see the deer earlier? There were about six or so of them in the back yard when I got home earlier."

"I saw them out the window before I jumped on a call. By the time I looked again, they were gone. They're so innocent looking and skittish. The slightest sound sends them scurrying away. I don't think I'll ever get sick of seeing animals out there, though. It's so beautiful here."

"It really is. I don't want to live anywhere else if I don't have to." Even though she'd grown up in Riston, Anna loved it there and had no desire to move.

"Why would you have to?" Ben asked.

"Well, it's a small town and only so many jobs available for recent college graduates. Even less for new lawyers. There's only one big law firm in town, and that's where my stepmother works. There's no way I'd go there."

Ben frowned. "Yeah, I can see how that would be awkward. There must be some smaller firms?"

"There are a few, but it's doubtful they'd need to hire additional lawyers. I suppose you never know, though. I have a few years before I have to really worry about it, anyway. So, how was your day?" Anna didn't want to think about the fact that she might not be able to start law school in the fall or work in Riston when she finished.

"My day was pretty great. A good friend agreed to sign on as the head writer and show runner for the TV project. He's flying in Sunday night for a few days and then he'll be back a week or so later to start working on the scripts. He's going to stay here for a few nights."

"Oh, that's great."

"I think you'll like him. His name is Adiel."

Just as Anna finished her soup, she saw Taylor stirring and went to give her a bath and a bottle. Ben took her and played with her for a while and Anna decided to check out the gym. She did the elliptical for a half hour and used free weights to tone her arms and legs. When she returned to the house, Ben was changing Taylor's diaper, and the baby was yawning and rubbing her eyes.

"She looks ready to go to bed. Do you want me to put her down?" Anna was still trying to get used to what her hours were. Ben had said she would have

Taylor during the day and he'd take over in the evenings, but she still felt like she should do more since she was there.

Ben grinned. "I've got it. It's my shift now. Once she's settled, I'm thinking about watching a movie if you feel like joining me."

"Sure. I'm going to take a quick shower and then I'll be out."

Taylor wasn't as tired as he'd thought. She seemed to catch a second wind and demanded that he read Good Night Moon again. He went to read one of the new books that Anna had bought that day but Taylor had burst into tears and said the one word she knew, 'no' repeatedly, until he picked up Good Night for a third time. Her eyes shut for good when he was halfway through, but he continued on anyway. By the time he closed the book, she was fast asleep.

Anna was waiting for him in the living room. Her hair was still damp as she sat cross-legged on the sofa in her turquoise blue sweats and white long-sleeved t-shirt. She was flipping through a magazine and looked up when he walked into the room.

"It took a little longer than I expected." He settled onto the sofa next to her and reached for the remote.

"Babies can be unpredictable." She smiled and he couldn't help but notice how it lit up her face.

"Have you seen the new Jack Raven movie?" Ben asked. He'd been looking forward to watching it as he'd missed seeing it in the theaters.

"No, not yet. I'd love to see it. I've seen all of his other movies."

"Great, I'll tee it up then." Ben found the movie on demand and for the next two hours they were on the edge of their seat, watching the suspense thriller. It had a twist ending that took them both by surprise.

"That was so good," Anna said as the credits rolled.

"I think it was even better than the last one," Ben agreed.

He clicked through the channels and there wasn't much of anything else on, so he settled on the news. He snuck a look at Anna. She looked so comfy. His leather sofa was soft and squishy and she was curled up in the corner of it with a fleece blanket tucked snugly around her. She surprised him by stretching slowly, then bouncing up and announcing, "I'm going to have a small bowl of ice cream. Do you want some?"

He laughed. "Yes, but make mine a big bowl."

Anna returned a few minutes later with two bowls of chocolate chip ice cream.

"This is one of the reasons I worked out earlier," she said as she handed him his bowl. "I saw Betty putting the groceries away, and this is my favorite flavor."

Ben inhaled his ice cream and set his empty bowl on the coffee table. Anna had barely made a dent in hers. She savored every small nibble. He found himself wanting to know more about her.

"Why law school?" he asked.

She looked up and considered the question. "It's something I've always known I wanted to do, for as long as I can remember."

"Do you know what kind of law you want to focus on?"

"I want to be a generalist. I know I'll have to work for a firm first, but someday, I'd love to open my own small office and do a little bit of everything. Whatever people need me to do."

"So you don't want to be a high powered criminal lawyer or a big corporate attorney? You'd have to move to a big city to do that."

Anna shook her head. "That doesn't appeal to me at all. What kind of law did you focus on?"

"I started out at a small law firm. I worked summers for one of my dad's friends. It was a small office, and we did just what you mentioned, a little bit of everything. I liked it. But after I graduated, I got an offer from a venture capital firm and after a few years there, I was ready for the role at Blue Sky Pages.

"Do you ever think you'd go back to practicing law?" Anna asked. It was a question he'd asked himself recently since he didn't need to spend as much time on Blue Sky issues.

"Maybe. As you said earlier, there's only a few law firms here. Maybe there's room for another. It wouldn't be anytime soon I don't think, though. I'm busy with a few different projects now, including the new TV show."

"You decided to invest?"

Ben nodded. "Yes, once Adiel said he was on board, I called Steven and told him I was in. He sent me a contract, and I'm going to look it over tonight and stop by his attorney tomorrow to drop off a check and the signed paperwork."

"That's exciting," Anna said.

Ben thought of something Wade had suggested to him when they met for lunch.

"Were you planning to go to trivia this week?" he asked.

"I'm not sure. I was hoping to, but I wasn't sure if it would work with the schedule. Everyone usually gets there around six and has pizza before trivia. I could always go a little bit later."

"Or we could go together. Betty babysits for me once or twice a week, depending what is going on. I could have her watch Taylor Thursday night. Wade said it would be a good way for me to meet more people here."

"It would be! It's really a fun night out."

"Okay, then. It's a date. Well, no, not a date, but you know what I mean?" Ben felt suddenly awkward, wishing it was a date, but knowing it couldn't be and not wanting Anna to get the wrong idea.

"I know what you mean." She smiled as if to assure

him that she hadn't taken it the wrong way. He was equally relieved and disappointed. Even though he knew it was a bad idea, part of him wanted her to be excited about an actual date with him. Which meant that he really should get out there and try to meet people.

CHAPTER 6

B en didn't stop the next day. He was busy from the moment he woke up. He had several early morning calls with people on the East Coast, which meant his first conference call was at six a.m. By noon, he was fried, and more than ready to get out of the house and take a drive into town to his bank and then the law firm to drop off a check and a signed contract for Steven. He'd been too busy to stop for lunch and his stomach was protesting as he drove. He decided to swing by Kelsey's Kafe for lunch after he left the law firm.

He parked and a moment later, a sleek champagne-colored Mercedes sedan pulled in next to him. The car looked as if it had just been driven off the lot, it was so new. As he walked toward the door, he noticed the driver of the Mercedes getting out of the car. A pair of slim legs on dangerously high heels hit the ground first, followed by an elegant older woman with a perfectly shaped blonde bob. He walked in the door and the woman rushed in behind him.

"You must be Ben Turner!" she exclaimed and held out her hand. "I'm Elise Cummings, the office manager. Ray is expecting you. You can go right into the conference room.

"Okay, thanks."

Ben met with Ray briefly, dropped off his check and contract, and was eager to be on his way to grab lunch. He liked Ray Thompson. Ray was an older man who'd founded the firm years ago and didn't waste a lot of time on small talk. They chatted for a few minutes and then both men were ready to go. But Elise wasn't ready to let him escape just yet. She was waiting at the front desk as he walked by.

"Ben, if you have a moment?"

He paused, hoping it would just be a moment.

"I just wanted to welcome you to Riston. I think it's really special that you're raising your sister's daughter here." She smiled big, and he forced a smile in return. There was nothing special about what he was doing. It was just what you did for family. It was Taylor who was special. In the short time she'd been with him, she'd captured his heart and he couldn't imagine her not being with him.

"Thank you." Another thought occurred to him.

"I think we pulled in at the same time earlier. Your car is gorgeous. Is it new?"

Elise looked thrilled at the compliment. "Yes! Thank you. It's a special edition, and I got a nice discount because I paid cash. I imagine you pay cash all the time?" Ben tried not to laugh. She really was a piece of work.

"Oh, look at the time. I have to run. It was nice talking with you!" He dashed out the front door while Elise was still talking. And as he drove away he couldn't help thinking how interesting it was that someone who supposedly didn't inherit much at all was paying cash for a new Mercedes. Before he said anything to Anna, though, he wanted to dig around a bit more and see what he could find out.

BEN ARRIVED at Kelsey's Kafe a few minutes past one. The dining room was busy, but there was plenty of room at the counter. He sat down next to an older couple who were bickering about what to order.

"Simon, I know you want the burger with everything, but you know what the doctor said. That's okay once in a while, but you need to watch the fatty food. Get the toasted turkey sandwich or a bowl of soup." Her tone was sweet but bossy and Ben smiled as he listened, picturing his own parents saying similar things.

"Fine, I'll have the blasted turkey sandwich. Jaclyn, I swear you're not as much fun as you used to be."

"I am the queen of fun! But I'm planning on you sticking around for a few more years, so you need to do your part."

"Hmmmm..." The older gentleman picked up the newspaper by his elbow and started fiddling with the crossword puzzle as a pretty young waitress with long brown hair in a ponytail came to take their order. After she finished with them, she turned her attention to Ben, and handed him a menu.

"Hi, there. Can I get you something to drink?" He noticed that her slightly askew name tag read 'Rachel'.

"Sure. I'll have a root beer and Bob's famous burger." He felt a little guilty ordering it with the older gentleman sitting two stools down, but he'd been craving a burger since Wade told him it was the best thing on the menu, other than the specials.

"Good choice." She returned a moment later and set down a tall glass of root beer.

"Thanks, Rachel."

She looked startled by him mentioning her name and he could tell she was wondering if she was supposed to know him. He tapped his chest, the spot on her uniform where her name tag was, and she laughed.

"We just started wearing these, and I forgot it was even there." Something buzzed in her apron and Rachel pulled out her cell phone to check a text message. She looked dazed as she put the phone back in her pocket.

"Is everything okay?" Ben asked.

"What? Oh, yes. Everything is great. Really great, actually." She took a step closer and spoke softly. "I just heard that there is going to be a TV pilot filmed here in Riston. My agent is going to send my information in to see if I can get a meeting."

That piqued Ben's interest. "What do you do?"

"I'm an actress. I know Riston isn't exactly the best place to be for that, but for family reasons, I can't move for a few years. This is the biggest opportunity that has come along so far."

"Have you done any acting?" Rachel was a very pretty girl, and probably photogenic on-screen but that was no guarantee she had any acting talent.

"Just local productions, mostly. Theater stuff and a commercial last year for an organic toothpaste product."

"Are you in anything now?"

"We saw Rachel last night at the Spire downtown. Rachel was a marvelous Blanche!" the older woman sitting next to him said.

She then leaned forward, "Couldn't help but over-hear. I'm Jaclyn and this is Simon. We usually come in for breakfast but today is our weekly lunch visit."

So this was the famous Jaclyn. "It's a pleasure to meet you both."

Ben turned his attention back to Rachel. "You're starring in A Streetcar Named Desire? That's quite a play."

Rachel smiled. "It's incredible. I feel very lucky to be part of it."

"How much longer is it booked for?"

"Sunday night is our last performance."

Ben thought for a moment. Adiel was flying in Sunday afternoon. If he was up for it, they could check out the play, and Rachel's performance. As show runner, Adiel would be heavily involved in casting.

"I have a friend coming into town this weekend. He loves going to plays, so we'll try to make it to one of the shows."

Rachel looked thrilled. "Oh, I hope you do. That would be great!" She turned as Bob hollered her name to pick up food.

"I know what you're doing, and I approve," Jaclyn said.

Ben looked at the sweet, white-haired lady sitting next to him and wondered what on earth she was talking about. He decided to play along.

"Well, I'm glad you approve, but what is it you think I'm doing?"

Jaclyn leaned forward and whispered so only Ben could hear.

"You don't want to get that girl's hopes up, so you're not telling her about your involvement with the show. You want to go to the play and see for yourself if she might be right for it."

Ben was stunned. Very few people knew of his

involvement and he'd only just made it official less than an hour ago. He didn't quite know what to say.

"I'm right, aren't I?" Jaclyn looked delighted with herself as Rachel delivered Simon's soup and Jaclyn's salad.

"You are. But how did you know that?"

Jaclyn smiled. "I just know things. You probably won't believe me when I say the fairies told me, but they did. They're quite excited about it."

"The fairies?"

Jaclyn sighed. "Yes, dear. I knew you'd have a hard time with that. But it is what it is. Oh, you might want to bring your nanny to the play, too. She loves the theater."

"You know Anna?" Ben hadn't even thought about inviting Anna. Saturday and Sunday were her days off, but maybe she'd want to join them.

"Yes, I know her. She's Tammy's friend, the gal that manages the bookstore with Melissa. They both come to trivia often." Jaclyn gave Ben a long look, and then said, "Maybe you should come to trivia, too. It might be a nice way to meet everyone."

Ben smiled, as Rachel set his burger down. "Wade suggested that, too. Anna and I are planning to go this week."

"Good, good."

Ben started eating his burger, which was as outstanding as Wade had promised it would be. His cellphone buzzed when he was almost done eating with a reminder that he had a conference call at two. If he left now, he'd just about make it on time. He motioned to Rachel that he was ready for a check and put cash down for it as soon as she brought it over.

Jaclyn and Simon were still eating and Jaclyn was yakking away while Simon kept stealing glances at his crossword puzzle. They looked up when he stood to go.

"Nice chatting with you both," Ben said as he picked up his car keys.

"Nice to meet you, too, young man," Simon said.

"We'll see you at trivia dear. Oh and please do put in a word for me if you wouldn't mind. I'd love to be an extra on that show. Both Simon and I would."

"What?" Simon said as if it was the first time he'd heard of it.

"We talked about this. You don't have to say anything. It's right up your alley."

"Hmm."

Ben smiled. "I'll see what I can do."

CHAPTER 7

"Thanks so much for babysitting tonight, Betty." Anna was looking forward to going to trivia and introducing Ben to her friends—other than Wade who he already knew.

"I'm happy to do it. Ben doesn't take me up on it often enough. It's good for him, for both of you, to get out and about."

Anna was in the kitchen, sitting at the island and chatting with Betty while she chopped carrots and celery for a casserole she was making. Taylor was dozing and Anna figured she had time for a quick cup of Caramel Shortbread tea. She'd offered to make Betty a cup, too, but she declined, until she smelled it.

"What is that?" she'd asked.

"It's one of the teas I ordered from David's Teas. They have really fun flavors."

"Alright, I'll have a cup."

"So, you seem as though you're settling in nicely. Are you liking the job?" Betty asked as she took her first sip of the tea.

"Yes, it's working out even better than I'd hoped. I'd never actually worked as a nanny before," she admitted.

Betty looked surprised to hear it. "Well, you could have fooled me."

"I was upfront with Ben. I didn't think I had enough experience for him, but I have done my share of babysitting and have younger siblings. Plus, Taylor and I got along pretty well in the coffee shop and all the other nannies bombed. So I was his best, maybe his only option."

Betty nodded. "You are good with Taylor. Everything happens for a reason," she said as she looked toward the large window that looked out on the backyard. Anna followed her gaze. The deer were back, even more of them this time. Anna counted eleven.

"I never get tired of seeing them," Betty said.

Anna nodded. "There's something magical about them." One of the deer looked up at that moment and cocked its head. The sweet, innocent look on its face was endearing. But then, suddenly they all turned and ran away. Something had spooked them. A moment later, they saw what it was. A giant moose casually strolled through the backyard. They watched as it looked around and then disappeared into the woods behind the house.

"And this is why I don't want to move," Betty said.

Anna agreed. She finished her tea and thought about how well her new job was working out so far. She and Taylor and Ben had fallen into a comfortable routine. After dinner, Anna visited Ben's gym above the garage and then relaxed with Ben watching TV. They'd started working their way though all eight seasons of Seinfeld the night before, watching four episodes back to back and laughing and chatting for hours. He was easy to talk to, and they seemed to share the same taste in what they liked to watch. They were becoming good friends, and she was happy about that.

More than once she'd had to remind herself that anything more than friends was off-limits and that she should not be so attracted to her employer. It was hard not to be, though. Ben ticked all the boxes—fun, nice, and extremely good-looking. But she knew if they ever crossed the friendship line that her working relationship wouldn't be nearly as comfortable and she didn't want to do anything to jeopardize that. Plus, she'd never even gotten the slightest hint that Ben saw her as anything other than the nanny, so she was being silly, anyway.

"Penny for your thoughts?" Anna jumped at the sound of Ben's voice. He'd walked into the kitchen and she hadn't even heard him coming. Out of the corner of her eye, she also saw Taylor stirring.

"Hey, there. Taylor's awake. I was just going to feed her before we head out."

A half-hour later, with Taylor fed and happily playing with Betty, Anna and Ben headed off to the restaurant at the ranch for trivia night.

Ben drove, and they chatted easily about their days as they rode along. Less than twenty minutes later, they arrived at River's End Ranch and walked into the restaurant. Jaclyn and Simon were already there at their usual big, round table. Wade, his wife Maddie and their nine-year-old daughter Vivian were there, too.

"Vivian has been dying to come to trivia. But we're not staying for the whole game, just the first half. Someone has school tomorrow."

Vivian pouted. "I can totally stay up."

"Oh, I have no doubt that you can. But I also know you'll be too tired tomorrow morning. So, pizza and first half of trivia it is," Maddie said firmly and then laughed. She patted her stomach. She wasn't really showing yet as she wasn't due until May. "Even if she's not tired, I know I will be. I'm doing well enough to be off bedrest for now, so I don't want to push my luck."

Tammy arrived a few minutes later, along with Melissa and her husband Jack. Anna introduced everyone to Ben, except for Jack and Melissa, who he already knew. Melissa's sister, Melanie, and her husband Bryan arrived at the same time as Clark, the doctor Anna had met at trivia the week before.

"Clark and Bryan are brothers, and Melissa and Melanie are twins," she explained to Ben.

"Got it. I think."

Anna laughed. "I know it's a lot of names at once. I don't think anyone else is coming tonight, though."

"Good!"

"Melissa has some exciting news," Jack said once everyone's pizzas were served, and he had their full attention.

Melissa smiled. "It might not ever actually happen but The Final Letter has been optioned by a Hollywood production company."

"Congratulation! What does that mean exactly?" Jaclyn asked

"It means that they will be shopping my story around to a few different studios and hope they get the green light to develop a pilot episode for a mystery series."

"You mean like a True Detective kind of thing?" Simon asked.

"Yes, exactly."

"Well, that is amazing news," Wade asked.

"Which production company is it?" Ben asked.

"Ross Klein films," Melissa answered.

Ben nodded. "I haven't worked with them, but they have a great reputation. I'll have to check out your book. I love a good mystery/thriller."

"Melissa's story is so good. I couldn't even put it down," Jack said proudly.

As soon as they finished eating, Arthur, the trivia host, came around with pencils and pads of paper to write down their answers and keep score. They did well in the first half and even Vivian contributed a winning answer when the question was about children's literature. Anna was impressed that Ben contributed several winning answers, too, across varied categories—history, sports and even finance. As usual, Anna did best with the movie and entertainment questions. When Wade, Maddie and Vivian left, they were in first place.

Just as trivia was starting up again, Anna noticed a stunning tall woman with long, layered hair that was so light it was almost white. She looked vaguely familiar but Anna couldn't place where she'd seen her before. As the woman walked toward their table, she also noticed heads turning and a curious buzz in the air. She stopped when they reached their table, and stood by Ben and the empty seat next to him where Wade had been sitting.

"Hey, stranger. Is this seat taken?" Her voice was low and breathy and, again, oddly familiar.

Ben turned and Anna saw a look of shock cross his face. He stood and gave the woman a hug. "Sierra, what are you doing here? It's great to see you. Please, join us."

Her smile was dazzling as she looked around the table as she sat next to Ben.

"Everyone, this is Sierra Barker." He introduced everyone to her and Anna realized once he told them her full name, who she was. Sierra was a famous soap opera actress who was starting to branch out of the soaps. She was about Ben's age and from what Anna could remember, she was divorced a year or so ago. She seemed to know Ben very well.

She was friendly and everyone peppered her with questions, which she answered graciously. Jaclyn, as it turned out, was a big fan.

"I've watched Canyon Falls since the show started. You really should kick that Victor to the curb."

Sierra laughed. "I couldn't agree more."

"How long are you here?" Anna heard Ben ask. She leaned forward a little to better hear her answer.

"I'm not sure, exactly. A few days, a week maybe? It depends how my meetings with Steven go and the show runner. I'll be seeing him Monday or Tuesday."

Ben nodded and Anna noticed that he didn't mention Adiel's name, which she thought was interesting. She couldn't help wondering how Ben and Sierra knew each other. If they were just friends or if there was some kind of romantic history.

"So, will you show me the town while I'm here? I don't have any meetings until Monday."

Ben hesitated before answering but finally said, "Of course, I'd be happy to. I'm still new here myself, but I know a few places we could go."

"Great, here's my number. I have to run. I just saw the people I was supposed to meet over at the bar." She handed Ben a cocktail napkin with her phone number scrawled on it and then addressed the table. "So great to meet you all." And then she was gone.

"Well, wasn't that something," Jaclyn said and then she asked the question Anna was dying to know the answer to. "Old girlfriend of yours?"

Ben looked uncomfortable with the question. "We dated, a long time ago. She's a great girl."

"Hm," Jaclyn replied, before turning her attention back to the game at hand.

They were in first place going into the final question, but it was a hard one and they second-guessed themselves, changing their first answer—which turned out to be correct—and going with something else. And it was a close game, so they had bet it all and ended up in last place.

"Easy come, easy go," Simon said as their waitress dropped off the check. They usually all threw money into the pot, but Ben grabbed the check and handed it to the waitress with his card.

"You don't have to do that," Jack protested and the others all nodded.

"I know. But I'm happy to. I appreciate being included. Next time we'll win."

Everyone thanked him and as they left the restaurant, Anna saw that Sierra was gone, too. She wondered if Ben was looking forward to seeing more of Sierra while she was here. For some reason, she found the thought of the two of them depressing, yet she had to admit they made a handsome couple. Ben was tall and Sierra was just a few inches shorter instead of nearly a foot shorter, like Anna was. She sighed. It was just another sign that they weren't meant to be more than friends.

When they walked into the house, Ben put his arm on hers and she stopped to face him.

"I just wanted to thank you for bringing me along tonight. I had fun."

She smiled. "I'm glad. You're welcome to come anytime."

"I know you're off this weekend, but if you don't have plans Sunday night, would you like to join Adiel and me for dinner and a play? We're going to see Rachel, the waitress from Kelsey's Kafe star in A Streetcar Named Desire."

Anna hesitated. Who was Rachel? Was this another actress that Ben had dated or wanted to date?

"Is she a friend of yours?"

"No. I just met her today. She seems like a nice enough girl. She's interested in auditioning for the TV show so I thought it might be a good way for Adiel to assess if she's right for it."

Anna relaxed. "That sounds fun. I'd love to go."

CHAPTER 8

Ben yawned and stretched. It was nearly midnight and as much as he wanted their Seinfeld marathon to continue, he knew he had to call it quits. He glanced over at Anna and her eyes were half-shut, too. He smiled. It had been a perfect night as far as he was concerned. They'd had Chinese food delivered and enjoyed it with a few beers while they watched back-to-back episodes of Seinfeld and laughed all night.

Anna was on her side of the sofa and he was on his and it was just really comfortable. He frowned as he thought about his plans for Saturday night, which he was dreading. He knew it was the polite thing to do, to show Sierra around, but he wasn't looking forward to it. He almost invited Anna to join them, but sensed that neither woman would have been keen on that idea.

"Do you have any fun plans for the rest of the weekend?" he asked as he shut off the TV.

Anna yawned too before answering. "Tammy and I are doing something tomorrow night. I'm not sure what, maybe grabbing a bite to eat or seeing a movie. What about you?"

"I told Sierra I'd take her out. Any ideas on where we should go?"

Was he imagining it or did Anna not like the idea of him taking Sierra out, either?

"Well, it depends. Do you want a lot of attention or would you rather go somewhere out of the way?"

"I'm sure Sierra would love the attention. But I'd prefer to go to somewhere no one will notice us. I'm trying to keep a low profile here."

"You could try the Belfry. It's more upscale and much smaller. A special occasion kind of place."

"That's not a bad idea. Is the food good?"

Anna laughed. "I've never been there. Like I said, it's a special occasion restaurant and a bit out of my price range."

"Got it. Thanks for the suggestion, then. And we're on for Sunday, though? The play with Adiel?"

Anna smiled. "I'm looking forward to it."

ANNA WALKED into the kitchen Saturday night just as Ben was saying goodbye to Taylor and Betty.

"You look great for your big date," she teased him.

"Trust me, it's not a big date," he said. But he did look great. He was wearing a hunter green sweater over a white t-shirt and well-made pants. The green brought out the green flecks in his eyes. She looked away, hating that she was feeling jealous about his night out with Sierra. She had no right to feel that way.

"Have fun with Tammy," he said as they reached their cars.

She followed him out of the driveway as she headed to Tammy's house. They saw a romantic comedy they'd both been dying to see, and then went to the Mexican restaurant in the middle of Main Street to share an order of loaded nachos and have some margaritas.

"You like this guy," Tammy announced when Anna finished telling her about Ben's date with Sierra.

"I may have a crush on him. I know it's stupid." Anna took a sip of her margarita and savored the sweet tartness of it.

"I don't think it's stupid. He's single, too. I know he's your boss, but if the two of you get along as well as it seems—well, maybe it could be more?"

Anna sighed. "I can't risk doing anything to screw up this job. The money is too important."

Tammy frowned. "What's going on with that? Have you applied for financial aid yet?"

"I looked into it. I'm pretty much screwed. Elise said she won't help me and I'm pretty sure I wouldn't qualify for much anyway based on what my father made."

"But I thought you said Elise told you there wasn't much left? Maybe you could qualify for some aid."

"I hate the thought of asking her for anything." Although it had crossed her mind to at least talk to Elise and see if she would fill out her part of the financial aid application.

"Speak of the devil. She's coming this way. You can ask her."

Anna looked up and sure enough, Elise was walking toward them, no doubt on her way to the restroom that was just beyond where they were sitting. Elise stopped in surprise when she saw Anna.

"I thought you'd left town."

"No, I'm still here. I just got a job and started working."

"What kind of a job?"

Anna hesitated, knowing her answer wouldn't go over well. "I'm a live-in nanny, actually."

Elise raised her eyebrows. "You? That's rich. Must be someone new to town?"

Anna just nodded. She had no intention of telling Elise who she worked for.

"I'm glad I ran into you, though. Would it be possible for me to drop off my financial aid application sometime this week? There's a section that you need to fill out."

"You're still planning on law school? I told you

before, there's no point to my filling that out because you won't qualify for aid."

"But, I thought you said Dad didn't leave you with much?"

A strange look crossed her face, and she hurriedly said, "That's right, he didn't. But he still has that Amazon stock. I promised him I wouldn't sell it, but it's probably worth enough that you won't qualify for aid. I'm sorry to say. I have to go now...take care."

Anna watched her totter away on her high heels and shook her head.

Tammy was livid. "What an utter bitch! She should just give you that money for law school. You really should fight her for it."

Anna was angry, too, but more deflated than anything. She'd hoped that maybe Elise would want to help her. But instead, she just reinforced how much she hated her.

"Forget about her. The nachos are here...let's dig in."

ANNA GOT HOME a few minutes past eleven and relieved Betty. Taylor was fast asleep and Anna was wide awake. She didn't expect Ben home anytime soon. She knew they were going to that fancy restaurant, and she was pretty sure Sierra would want to go somewhere fun afterwards, maybe to hear some music at a local bar where she would be sure to be recognized. Though she knew Ben didn't want that, but still, she couldn't imagine Sierra being satisfied with just dinner. She'd made it clear that she wanted Ben to show her around the town.

Between running into Elise and picturing Sierra in Ben's arms on the dance floor, Anna was feeling pretty down. Maybe a bit of chocolate chip ice cream would help. Not that she was hungry in the least. But eating was rarely about hunger for her. Anna had always been a stress eater and ice cream was considered comfort food for a reason.

She'd just settled herself at the island counter with a cup of hot herbal tea and a rather large bowl of ice cream, when the front door opened and Ben walked in.

"You're still up." He sounded both surprised and pleased. He glanced at her ice cream and then walked toward the freezer. "Did you save any for me?"

Anna nodded. "There's enough for another good-sized bowl."

Ben pulled out the carton and grabbed a spoon from a drawer. He didn't even bother with a bowl. He settled into the seat next to her and took a big bite.

"I didn't think you'd be home so early," Anna said.

Ben smiled. "If it was up to Sierra, I wouldn't be. She wanted to go to Figs and go dancing after we ate. That was the last thing I felt like doing."

"How did you get out of it?" Anna was curious as Sierra seemed like the determined type.

"Well, I'm not proud to admit it, but I used Taylor. Having a baby comes in handy sometimes. I told her I had to get back to relieve her sitter."

"Well done."

"How about you? How was your night?"

"It was fun, until we ran into Elise at the Mexican restaurant."

"Did she give you a hard time?"

"She did, but it was my fault. I made the mistake of thinking she might actually help me. I asked if she'd fill out her part of the financial aid form, and she said no."

"Why?"

"She said there was no point to it, that I wouldn't qualify for aid because of my Dad's income or rather his stock account. But she promised she wouldn't touch that money, so it is what it is."

"That doesn't sound right. I'm happy to look into this for you, as your attorney."

Anna was tempted but didn't want to make a fuss.

"I don't want to do that to Hayley and Tommy. It could get ugly if we get lawyers involved, and it's too soon after my father passed. I'll find a way somehow."

Ben looked like he wanted to push the matter, but just sighed and finished his ice-cream instead. Finally he said, "Well, if you change your mind, let me know."

"I will." Anna took the last bite of her ice cream, rinsed the bowl and put it in the sink. Suddenly she was bone tired and ready to fall into bed. "I'm heading to bed. Goodnight, Ben."

Ben dropped his empty container into the trash and pulled Anna in for a comforting hug. He released her a moment later and brushed a wayward strand of hair off her face.

"Everything will work out, Anna. Don't give that woman another thought. Sleep tight."

"Thanks, I appreciate it." Anna padded off to bed still feeling the warmth of Ben's hug. It had been comforting and something else, at the same time. And she only wished it had lasted longer.

CHAPTER 9

B en was up early with Taylor the next day. He was in the kitchen feeding her breakfast when Anna came by in her workout clothes on the way to the gym. Taylor got excited when she saw her and Anna stopped over to drop kisses on her head and chat with her for a few minutes.

"Enjoy your workout," he called after her as she stepped outside. She looked so cute in her leggings and tank top. She didn't need to lose any weight, but he liked that she wanted to stay in shape. And he liked that she enjoyed food as much as he did. So many of the women he'd dated, especially the actresses and models, had strange diets. Pizza and ice cream were rarely allowed.

An hour later, Anna returned, glistening with sweat and in Ben's eyes, looking better than Sierra had the night before in her silk dress and high heels. She'd picked at her food at the fancy restaurant they went to and didn't seem to enjoy it at all. Though she'd enjoyed her wine well enough. And she hadn't been happy at all when he said he had to get home because of Taylor.

She'd pouted, and he'd been relieved when he dropped her off at her cabin at River's End Ranch. She tried to set another date, but he'd put his foot down this time and simply said he was busy and had company coming to visit. He didn't dare mention that it was Adiel or she would have insisted on all of them getting together. When she got out of the car and shut the door behind her, he felt nothing but relief and an eagerness to get home.

Anna came back into the kitchen a half hour later, freshly showered and with her hair blown dry and piled up in a French twist. She was wearing a pretty pink sweater and a long, cream-colored skirt and her caramel-colored cowboy boots.

"You look nice. Where are you off to?"

"Sunday service at the little church at River's End Ranch. It's a nice, intimate service and always puts me in a good mood to start the week off fresh." She smiled and Ben was tempted to join her, to bundle Taylor up and head to church, too. But, he knew that was too optimistic. Taylor was still teething and unpredictable. He didn't want to be a disruption.

"Maybe we'll join you sometime, when Taylor's teething settles down."

Anna smiled. "I'd like that."

After Anna left and Taylor went down for a nap, Ben was feeling restless. He had plenty of work he could do, but he felt like trying to cook. One thing he'd always loved when he lived at home was Sunday roast dinners after church. He wasn't much of a cook, but he thought he could manage cooking a chicken. He'd seen one in the fridge earlier. After googling instructions online, he heated the oven, stuck the chicken on a half sheet cooking pan, stuffed a cut lemon in its cavity and sprinkled some rosemary and thyme over the top and a smear of butter. A dash of salt and pepper and it was ready to go in the oven. He added a few big baking potatoes, too, and then slid the tray into the oven. He set the timer for a little over an hour and then went into his office for a bit. The timer was essential because it was too easy for him to lose track of time.

As it turned out, Taylor got his attention just before the timer went off. He put her in her high chair with some cut up pieces of fruit and then took the chicken out of the oven. The whole house smelled pretty amazing, if he said so himself. When the chicken cooled enough, he cut a little up for Taylor and she gave it the thumb's up. When she was just about done, Anna walked through the door and stopped short and sniffed.

"Was Betty here?"

He laughed. "I think that's a compliment. No, I cooked a roast chicken. Smells like it came out okay. Want to try some? I was just about to fix a plate."

"Sure."

Anna gave his cooking the thumb's up, too, and after they ate, she insisted on cleaning up while he changed Taylor's diaper. When she was all fresh and clean, he brought her into the living room to let her crawl around and play with some of her toys. Anna was sprawled out on the sofa, reading a magazine.

A few minutes later, his cell phone rang, but he'd left it in his office.

"I'll be right back." He ran to his office and as he suspected, it was Adiel, letting him know that he'd just landed and would be there in a little over an hour. He ended the call and as he was walking back to the living room, Anna called for him to hurry up.

"Ben, get in here!" There was something about her tone that made him move faster and when he reached the living room, he understood why.

"I think she's about to walk!" Anna said.

They both watched in wonder. Taylor swayed back and forth as she held onto the side of the coffee table, then took a step away, let go, walked two steps and fell down.

"Taylor, that was amazing!"

He turned to Anna. "I can't believe she just walked!"

Anna looked thrilled, too. "I know."

They spent the rest of the afternoon encouraging Taylor to do it again and again and she laughed as she tried to walk and then fell. She thought it was the funniest thing ever. And then she blew Ben's mind when she fell into Anna who was sitting cross-legged on the floor. She laughed delightedly and then pulled on Anna's hair and said, "Mama!" The only other world she'd mastered thus far was "No," which she did enjoy using. Her calling Anna 'Mama' both amused him and made him feel something else entirely. Something confusing that he couldn't quite figure out.

Taylor started to rub her eyes, a sign that she was about ready for a nap and Ben suspected she might be down for a while after her walking lessons. He put her down and tucked her in and headed back to the living room. Anna was in the kitchen getting a glass of water.

"That was really something special," she said softly.

Ben nodded. "It was. Walking and another word in the same afternoon."

"Felt kind of weird and nice, to be called 'Mama'," Anna said with a smile. She was leaning against the island and Ben felt drawn to her. She was looking at him in a way that he hadn't seen before. There was something in her eyes—interest, maybe an invitation? He wasn't sure, but he didn't stop to think about it. He pulled her close to him and he kissed her, softly at first, but then she leaned into him and he pulled his arms more tightly around her. They kissed like that, for a long time and then, finally, he leaned back and smiled.

"I kind of got caught up in the moment. I hope you don't mind?"

"Mind? No, I..." Anna was interrupted by a knock at the door. Ben realized it must be Adiel. He went to the door and let him in.

ANNA STOOD THERE IN SHOCK. She couldn't believe Ben had just kissed her and that she'd kissed him back, quite thoroughly. And now his friend was here, and they had to act as though everything was perfectly normal, like nothing had just happened. That her world hadn't just been tilted on its axis. Adiel was going to be staying with them for a few days, so Anna knew it wasn't likely that she and Ben would even have a chance to talk about the kiss, or what it meant until after he left.

"Anna, this is Adiel. He's a good friend of mine."

"A pleasure to meet you, Anna." Adiel held out his hand and Anna shook it. She instantly liked him. As they chatted, she discovered a calm friendliness and curiosity about him that she found engaging. He was a handsome man, but he had a very different look. Adiel was a little shorter, maybe five foot ten or so and had unruly hair that was a little too long and a little too wavy, but it suited him. He had big, dark eyes and Anna got the sense that he was always taking note of everything, absorbing the conversations and images around him. He wore big, black glasses that gave him a studious, creative look. She knew that he was very good at what he did. Ben had told her that he'd created and written films and TV shows that she'd watched and enjoyed immensely.

She visited with him for a little bit before excusing herself to let the two of them catch up. She went to her room to lay down for a bit and read, but after a few pages, she fell asleep and to her surprise, dozed for a few hours. She checked the time when she woke and realized she had just enough time to freshen up before they were due to leave for dinner and the show. She splashed water on her face, added a touch of mascara and a bit of blush and fixed her hair. She added a silk floral scarf in tones of pink and blue to match her sweater and dress her outfit up a bit.

Ben smiled when she joined them in the living room. Betty was already with Taylor, and Ben and Adiel looked ready to go.

"You look nice," Ben said. "Are you all set?"

"I'm ready."

The performance was at four so they decided to see the show and then grab dinner after.

"Have you seen A Streetcar named Desire, Anna?" Adiel asked.

"No. I've always wanted to, though."

He smiled. "You are in for a treat. It's one of my all-time favorite plays. And Stella is a big part."

"I have a good feeling about Rachel," Ben said.

Anna didn't think she knew who Rachel was but when the show started and she saw the woman playing the part of Stella, she recognized her as the waitress from the cafe. She hadn't ever had a real conversation with her, though, and had no idea she was interested in acting. She quickly forgot that it was Rachel playing the part and got lost in the story. And when it ended, she was exhausted in a good way. It was an incredible story and there was something really special about Rachel.

Ben looked impressed, too. "So what did you think?" he asked them both as they walked into the main lobby.

"I loved it," Anna said.

"It was good. Rachel was great. Good find, Ben." Adiel looked pleased, as if he'd just discovered something that no one else knew about. Anna supposed that he had.

They waited in the lobby until the cast members came out and mingled in the crowd. When Rachel saw Ben, her eyes widened, and she walked over to them.

"You came!" She sounded pleased and surprised.

"I did. And I brought a few friends. Anna Kelley and Adiel Bozeman, this is Rachel."

"Rachel McIntyre," she said with a smile. "Thank you all so much for coming. I hope you enjoyed it."

"We did," Ben assured her. "We'll keep our fingers crossed for the opportunity you mentioned."

"Thank you! My agent hasn't heard anything yet, but he said the new show runner should be coming soon and then auditions would start."

"Good luck," Anna said.

Adiel winked. "If I have any say in it, the job is yours."

Rachel laughed. "Thank you."

As they walked away, Anna asked. "How come you didn't tell her who you are?"

"It's a little premature," Ben explained.

"Until I'm actually on board and have discussed budgets and actual casting needs with Steven, I don't want to get anyone's hopes up," Adiel said. "But I'd say there's an excellent chance that there will be a place for Rachel."

They decided to go to Figs for dinner. It had an eclectic menu and was right in the middle of Main Street. There was also a great blues band playing in the back of the restaurant and from where they sat, they could hear the music but it wasn't too loud and they could still hear each other talk, too.

Adiel was easy to talk to, and funny. He had them laughing with comical stories of things that happened on the set of his last TV show. They decided to just order a bunch of appetizers and stayed for several hours, drinking wine and sharing stories. Before she knew it, Anna had shared the whole sorry story of her evil stepmother, Elise, and the Amazon stock that was preventing her from getting financial aid.

"Do you know how many shares he had?" Adiel looked curious.

"Not that many, only about five hundred or so are

left. I haven't looked at the share price in a few years, but I know Elise said the price had dropped and he'd sold some. He had almost 1000 before that."

Ben and Adiel exchanged glances.

"I only know this because I own some Amazon stock, too, but it's gone way up in recent years. It always bounces around, but Anna, it's over $1200 a share now. If your father held on to 500 shares that's worth over $600,000."

"More than enough money for law school," Ben said. Anna could tell that he was furious on her behalf. She was stunned. And felt a bit foolish. It had never occurred to her to look up the price of that stock. She'd simply believed Elise when she'd said there wasn't much money left. She felt gullible and disgusted at Elise.

"Anna, will you please let me talk to her? I have an idea that won't cause a big fuss, but I think we should straighten this out," Ben said.

Anna nodded, feeling hopeful and nervous at the same time. She still had a lot at stake, if Elise told Ben the truth about what she'd done. But as long as he didn't share that Anna was working for him as a nanny, it might not come up. She crossed her fingers.

CHAPTER 10

Ben called the law firm where Elise Cummings worked first thing Monday. As he expected, she took his call eagerly.

"It's so nice to hear from you. How can I help you?"

"I have a matter I'd like to speak with you about. It shouldn't take long. Do you have a few minutes around lunch time today? I'm happy to come to your office, as I'll be in the area."

"Oh, of course, that would be wonderful. Did you want to talk to Ray, too?" She sounded excited and a little flustered, and Ben was counting on her not asking why he wanted to meet with her.

"No need to bother Ray. As I said, this should just take a few minutes. I'd like to talk with you."

"Oh, well, that's fine. Shall we say one o'clock?"

"I'll see you at one." Ben hung up and smiled. Elise

wouldn't expect the topic of the conversation to be Anna, which was exactly the way he wanted it. So she would be slightly off-guard.

He pulled into the lot at one sharp and saw her Mercedes parked right in front. When he walked into the law firm, the friendly young receptionist smiled and told Ben that Elise would be right out. He didn't even have a chance to sit before she was in the lobby to greet him and was all smiles.

"Let's go into the conference room. Can I get you coffee or tea?"

"No, thank you."

Once they were in the room with the door shut behind them, Elise leaned forward, radiating curiosity. "What can I help you with, Ben?"

"Well, first I'd like to thank you for meeting with me on such short notice," he said and smiled in a way that he'd been told women often found charming.

"I'm here on behalf of Anna Kelley." He let that sink in for a moment and it was like a shade was drawn and the welcoming smile was instantly with drawn.

"I don't understand?" There was ice in her tone and wariness.

"Anna has become...a good friend," he began. "She shared with me that she'd been accepted to law school but was having some issues financially. She said that you declined to help her with her financial aid application. Is that true?"

"Yes, well—yes, it is. I'm afraid that Anna won't

qualify for financial aid, so there's no point to filling out that application."

"I see. So, does that mean you'll just be writing a check for her tuition, then?"

Elise gasped. "No, of course not!"

Ben made a show of scratching his chin. "Well, I'm a little confused, then. If there's too much money for financial aid, then why isn't Anna seeing any of it?"

"Well," Elise stammered, clearly flustered. "It's just that there's no cash, you see. It's tied up in stock and 401ks, that kind of thing. Her father had a stock he loved, and I promised not to sell it."

"I see. Well, the 401k is irrelevant, that doesn't affect financial aid. The stock might, though, so I can see your dilemma."

Elise relaxed a bit, and then Ben went in for the kill.

"See, here's the thing. It's my understanding that Anna's father's will clearly left her a certain percentage of that stock and she was intending to use that for her education. Is that correct?"

"Yes, but—well, he made some changes to his will. So, that is no longer the case."

"Are you saying he cut his daughter out of the will? Why would he have done that?"

Elise stayed silent and looked away.

"You lied to him, didn't you? You told him that Anna got scholarships and didn't need the money and he was confused, his brain wasn't working the way it normally did anymore. And you took advantage of that?"

Elise sat up straight and stuck her chin in the air, a final attempt to bluff her way out of it. "You can't prove that!"

Ben sighed. "Elise. Before, I used to be a very good lawyer. I still am. If we were to take this to trial, you will lose. I can assure you of that. I have unlimited resources and you could burn through all the money you were left. I'm sure you don't want to do that, especially when you have zero chance of winning. It's a fairly simple matter to prove when your husband's cognitive skills began to decline and when I show that you cut his daughter out of the will then, based on lies —well, I think you know what will happen."

Elise said nothing. She just sat there fuming.

"Are you aware, Elise, of the current price of the Amazon stock?"

"No, I never paid much attention to that. Frank always handled his brokerage accounts."

"What was it the last time you checked?" he persisted.

"Around two hundred a share, maybe? I know he sold half of his stock. There's only about 500 shares left now."

"The stock has gone up a bit since then. It's worth an extra thousand dollars a share." He let that sink in and watched her mentally do the math.

"It's worth over $600,000?"

"It is. So, it won't be so painful now to give Anna her fair share, will it? I've taken the liberty of drafting an agreement letter for you to sign. If I can get your signature here, I'll drop this off at the bank today."

Elise sighed. "I suppose I don't really have a choice, do I?"

"Not from where I'm sitting, you don't." Ben smiled and handed her the pen.

She signed it and slid the paper over to him.

"How do you know Anna?" she asked.

"She's working as my live-in nanny," he said.

Elise crossed her arms and stared at him. "She's working as your nanny? I don't suppose she told you what she did to my son? A nanny is the last thing Anna should be."

A chill ran up Ben's spine.

"What are you talking about?"

"She almost killed my Tommy. It's a miracle he's alive today. She dropped him on his head!"

Ben stared at her in disbelief.

"Yes, it's true. Ask her yourself. I'm sure that didn't come up when she interviewed with you."

"I'm sure, if that is true, that she didn't mean to do it." He couldn't imagine Anna hurting a child.

"She was careless, in a hurry. Yes, of course it was an accident, but it never should have happened at all. It was completely preventable. I'd think long and hard about keeping her on if it were my child."

Ben stood. "Well, thank you for your time."

"Good day. I hope not to see you again any time soon."

Ben left, stopped by Anna's bank and dropped off the paperwork for Elise to transfer funds into Anna's account. He was glad he'd gotten Elise to agree to give Anna the money she deserved, but he was concerned about what she'd said about Anna.

Anna was feeding Taylor in the kitchen when Ben walked in. She couldn't read his expression at all and couldn't explain why but she had a sense of foreboding that something had gone very wrong.

"I need to talk to you, but need to return a few calls first. I'll be back in about twenty minutes." Ben disappeared into his office and Anna felt a pit grow in her stomach, a sinking feeling that got worse as the clock ticked. She finished feeding Taylor and put her down for a nap. Ben was due to come out of his office any minute and she was a bundle of nerves. He'd said he was going to talk to Elise and by his tone, she suspected he'd learned the truth. Or rather Elise's version of the truth. She made herself a cup of strong black coffee and stirred a little sugar in it as she sat waiting in the kitchen. Betty had gone shopping and wasn't due back for probably another half hour or so, so the house was quiet.

Finally, she heard footsteps coming her way. Ben

sat next to her at the island and his face was still hard to read.

"I went to see Elise."

Anna nodded and waited for him to continue.

"We had a good discussion about the will and that Amazon stock. We came to an understanding that she will give you the original amount you were due before she changed your father's will."

Anna was surprised. "You got her to agree to that?"

He shrugged. "I explained how it was in her best interest to honor that original will. I told her if we took her to court, the one she changed would not stand and it would cost her a lot of money."

"I see. Well, I can't thank you enough."

"You're very welcome. She also told me something else. Something that was disappointing to hear."

Anna looked away. She knew what was coming.

"Is it true? What she said?"

Anna faced him. "Yes, it's true. I dropped my little brother on his head. And it was awful. I still have nightmares about it. We were on our way out and Elise asked me to get Tommy. He was in his car carrier and it was sitting on the kitchen table. We were in a hurry. I picked it up fast, and it wasn't locked into position. It swung forward and Tommy toppled out, onto the hard wood floor. Onto his head."

"Oh, my God."

As they always did, the tears came as Anna told him the rest of the story. "We called 911, and they brought him into the local ER immediately, but his injury was too severe and his brain was swelling so fast. They had to helicopter him to Children's Hospital in Lewiston and it was touch and go for several weeks. He needed multiple surgeries to relieve the swelling on his brain."

"He's okay now?"

Anna nodded. "Yes. But it was a horrible year. The Children's Protective Services all but accused Elise of hurting Tommy on purpose. Because of his head injuries, they said it could have been caused by throwing him to the ground. It was horrible. They finally believed that I did it, though, and that it was just an accident."

Ben was looking at her curiously. "You said the carrier wasn't locked when you picked it up. Wouldn't that have been Elise's responsibility?"

Anna sighed. "Yes and no. She should have made sure it was locked and I should have checked that it was locked. We were both in a rush. It was truly an accident. But Elise has never forgiven me. Honestly, I don't think she's ever forgiven herself, either. She's just very lucky he's fine now. Of course, he can't play any contact sports, no football ever."

"A small price to pay. She asked me if you told me about this before I hired you."

"Would you have hired me if I had?" Anna said.

Ben sighed. "No, probably not. I don't like that you lied to me though, Anna."

Anna felt the tears threaten to fall again.

"I'm sorry. I really am."

They both turned at the sound of the front door opening. Adiel was back. Anna couldn't face him or anyone else at the moment.

"I'm going to my room."

ANNA SAT in her room and stewed for about twenty minutes. The look on Ben's face had cut right through her. She was so grateful for what he'd done and so sorry that she had turned out to be such a disappointment to him. Especially after the kiss they'd shared the other night, too. They still hadn't talked about that. But Anna had been thinking about little else.

And unfortunately there only seemed to be one sensible solution. She had to leave. She wasn't a hundred percent sure because she'd never been in love before, but she thought that she might be falling in love with Ben. And how could that ever work out? She was his nanny. And if he didn't feel the same way it would only be awkward for her to stay. It was highly inappropriate, to say the least. And yet, she kept replaying their kiss over and over.

It wasn't just the kiss, though. She knew she was going to miss Ben. She'd never been happier than she had since she'd been living there, spending time with him, and Taylor and Betty. They almost felt like a family. She enjoyed his company so much—too much. Just watching Seinfeld and eating ice-cream together and playing with Taylor. It was just perfect, and she was going to miss it horribly. But it was best for her to make a clean break. Let him find a nanny that wasn't going to go and fall in love with him and one that he wouldn't have to worry about with his daughter.

She called Tammy and asked if she could come and stay with her for a few days. She said she'd explain when she got there and Tammy didn't ask any questions, just told her she could stay as long as she needed to. She packed an overnight bag and planned to come back and get the rest of her luggage. It would be too awkward to move everything out now, with Adiel still visiting. She didn't want a scene, and she didn't want to embarrass Ben in front of his friend.

Adiel looked her way when she walked out to the kitchen and his eyes fell on her overnight bag. She put on a bright smile and tried to act as though everything was perfectly normal.

"I'm going to stay with my friend Tammy tonight. I'll be back in the morning. Adiel it was great to meet you."

"You, too. I hope to see you again soon." He gave her a big hug and his warm eyes that saw so much were full of sympathy.

Ben looked sick to his stomach.

"I'll walk you out."

He walked her out to her car and as soon as they

got outside asked, "What's going on? Why are you going to Tammy's?"

"I think it's probably best if you find a new nanny. Tammy said I can stay with her until I find my own place. Now, thanks to you, I'll have money to do that soon."

"You don't have to do this."

"I think I do. I'll come back tomorrow to get the rest of my stuff."

"But what about the other night? We kissed. We haven't talked about that yet."

"That's part of it, too, Ben. I liked that a little too much. I can't do that and be your nanny, too. It's not fair to any of us."

"We'll talk tomorrow," Ben promised.

Anna sat in her car for a moment and waited until she calmed down enough to drive. Her emotions were all over the place.

Tammy had the door open for her when she walked up. She pulled Anna in for a hug, and the tears came again, harder and faster this time.

"It's Ben, isn't it? Come on in."

"SHE'S NOT JUST the nanny, is she?" Adiel asked softly when Ben walked back in the house.

He sighed. "It's complicated."

"Is it? I've never seen you so comfortable or relaxed

with someone. She seems great. So what if she's your nanny? Life is short."

"She is great. I just found out something today, though, that threw me for a loop."

"Something about Anna?"

"Yeah. Something she didn't tell me that I heard from someone else first."

"How bad could it be?"

Ben told him what Anna had shared and about his meeting with Elise and Adiel sat quietly, taking it all in. Finally, he asked, "If you were in Anna's shoes, would you have shared that information with a potential new employer?"

Ben didn't have to think long about that. "No, probably not."

"So, you're just mad that you heard it from someone else first. And she's done a great job with Taylor from what you've said and from what I can see."

Ben nodded.

"But now you have feelings for her, and you're not sure what to do about it?"

"That's sums it up."

"That's a tough one. Do you want her to be your nanny? Or your girlfriend? It's not really possible to have both, is it?"

"I don't know."

Adiel slapped him on the back. "You have a lot to think about. I hope it turns out the way you both want it to."

CHAPTER 11

A nna got up early the next day and drove over to Ben's house just before ten. She woke up feeling sure of her decision to leave the nanny position and get her luggage. It was the only sensible thing to do. Then she and Ben could move on and he could find a nanny that wouldn't fall in love with him.

When she arrived, Betty was in the kitchen and smiled when she saw her.

"Ben's in his office. He said to tell you to go in as soon as you got here."

"Thanks, Betty."

Anna took a deep breath and slowly opened Ben's door. She peeked inside and he was on the phone but waved her in. A moment later he ended the call.

"Hey, there. I had a feeling you might come by early. Have a seat."

Anna sat in a padded leather armchair across from him. She looked around his office. It was a gorgeous room, and it suited him. There was a fire going in the corner and the walls were covered with bookcases, filled with books of all kinds.

"So, what are you thinking?" he asked gently.

She smiled sadly. "I've loved working here for you and Taylor and with Betty, but I think it's probably best if I move on and you find another nanny."

"Why do you think that's best?" Ben's voice cracked.

"You know why."

Ben shook his head. "I was upset about what I heard yesterday from Elise, but it just threw me. I understand why you didn't mention it and I don't care. I know you would never do anything to hurt Taylor."

"Thank you. I still think it's best, though, if you found another nanny."

"Why? Because we kissed?"

Anna nodded.

"Are you saying that you have feelings for me? Because I definitely do for you. I know this has happened fast, but I've always heard that when love finds you, you'll know it. It will feel right. Since I've met you, everything has felt right. I look forward to spending my nights with you and Taylor, hanging out watching Seinfeld, trying to cook a chicken, eating ice cream together in the kitchen and just kissing you. I've never been happier."

"I feel the same way," Anna said.

"But the problem is I don't want you to just be my nanny. I want more than that. And that's not fair to ask of you."

Anna's hopes sunk. She prepared herself to say goodbye to Ben, to get her luggage and move on. She tried as hard as she could to keep the tears from coming.

"So, I thought, if you possibly felt the same way that I do, maybe there was another way." Ben opened his desk drawer and pulled out an old, faded box. It was very small and made of black velvet. He opened it and pulled out an antique diamond ring.

"This was my grandmother's ring. She gave it to me years ago before she died and told me to give it to the girl I fell in love with. She said it was a lucky ring as it gave her over fifty years of marriage."

Ben got down on his knee and held up the ring.

"I know this is crazy, but it feels right to me. I hope it does to you. Anna, will you marry me? I can promise you a lifetime of ice cream and movies and love."

"Are you serious? Yes!"

Anna leaned in and wrapped her arms around Ben's neck and kissed him tenderly.

"Are you sure?" she asked when they finally came up for air.

"I've never been more sure of anything in my life."

EPILOGUE

Two weeks later, on a Sunday morning, Anna sat in church feeling very grateful. Although she'd been a little nervous when Ben proposed, it was only because it happened so fast, not because she was unsure of her feelings. They'd decided to get married quietly, the Saturday before Valentine's day, which was only a few weeks away. She was looking forward to it because once the initial shock of the proposal had passed, they'd settled in and just been so happy ever since.

Betty was thrilled for both of them and even Taylor seemed to approve, if that was possible. Ben thought she was just in a good mood because her teeth didn't seem to be bothering her as much, but Anna talked to her all the time and told her they were getting married. She liked to think the little girl understood more than they knew.

It was their first time bringing Taylor to church—and so far, so good. They sat in the back pew, just in case they needed to make an early exit. She stirred and whimpered a little just as the service was ending, but no one noticed. Ben carried her out and handed her to Anna when he saw someone he needed to go talk to for a moment.

"Is that an engagement ring?" Anna looked up to see Elise standing there, with Hayley and Tommy by her side. The two children ran over to give Anna hugs and to look at Taylor, who was staring back at them with huge, curious eyes.

"It is," Anna said as Ben returned to her side and gave her a kiss.

Elise's jaw dropped.

"Nice to see you again, Elise," Ben said with a smile.

"The two of you are engaged?"

"We are. I'm the luckiest man in Riston. Don't you think?" Ben asked, and Anna loved him for it.

"Well, congratulations, then." Elise shook her head and added, "All that fuss and you're not going to law school after all. Guess you'll be having one of your own soon enough?"

Anna took a deep breath and tried not to let Elise get to her.

"I'm still going to law school. I start this fall."

Elise looked surprised. "Really? I would have thought you wouldn't bother with that now that you have your hands full." She looked meaningfully at Ben. "It's not like you'll need to work now."

"I wouldn't dream of denying Anna her education and the chance to pursue her dream job. We can always hire another nanny or have Taylor go to the Kids' Korral a few afternoons a week. It might be good for her to be around other children," Ben said.

"I might not have classes five days a week either, so we have lots of options." Anna was hoping to have a three-day-per-week schedule, but even if it was five days, it wouldn't be full days. She and Ben had talked about it and both were determined to make it work.

"The world sure is different these days," Elise muttered. But then she smiled. "I am happy for you, Anna. I wish the two of you well. Come on, Hayley and Tommy, we need to go."

Anna watched them walk away and smiled when Ben took her hand.

"I think that went well," he said.

Anna laughed. "I'm just glad that you're my family now, and Taylor, too, and Betty."

Ben leaned over and kissed her. It was tender and sweet, and Anna didn't want it to end. She knew she'd never get tired of kissing him.

"I don't think I've told you this yet today, but I love you," he said softly. "Are you ready to go home?"

"I love you, too. And yes, let's go home."

A NOTE FOR READERS

I hope you enjoyed Anna and Ben's story! Next up is Clark and Tammy's story, Teasing Tammy.

If you enjoyed Billionaire's Baby, you might like my newest release, Nashville Dreams. If you've read Cute Cowboy, you'll recognize Laura Scott, Lily's friend that she goes to visit in Nashville. This is Laura's story.

It's a much longer book, and a bigger story, spanning more years. It's a personal favorite of mine as it has a bit more drama and some fun twists and turns. Readers seem to be enjoying it! You can check out Nashville Dreams here on Amazon if you like!

IF YOU'D LIKE an email alert when I have a new release or special promotion, please join my newsletter list.

Oh, one last thing, if you have a moment to leave a review, even a short sentence or two helps new readers find our books, and is much appreciated. Thank you so much!

~Pam

ALSO BY PAMELA M. KELLEY

See all my books here, https://pamelakelley.com/

And please join my FB reader group. It's a wonderful bunch of avid readers and I love sharing covers early, and asking for input and do special giveaways only for the group.

ABOUT THE AUTHOR

Pamela M. Kelley lives in the historic seaside town of Plymouth, MA near Cape Cod and just south of Boston. She has always been a book worm and still reads often and widely, romance, mysteries, thrillers and cook books. She writes contemporary romance and suspense and you'll probably see food featured and possibly a recipe or two. She is owned by a cute little rescue kitty, Bella.

Keep in touch!
www.pamelakelley.com
pam@pamelakelley.com

Made in the USA
Monee, IL
09 December 2022

20182738R00083